"Miasha writes with the fatal stroke of a butcher knife. This book is raw material. Squeamish readers beware. You want proof? Just read the first page."

—Omar Tyree, bestselling author of *Boss Lady*

"Scandalous and engrossing, this debut from Miasha . . . shows her to be a writer to watch."

—*Publishers Weekly*

"An absorbing tale."

—*Booklist*

"Miasha's careful composition brags a fast-moving plot with the twists and turns showing up at just the right moment. . . . This story made me gasp, made me shake my head, and brought forth a level of insight I never thought possible."

—Rawsistaz.com

"Miasha cooks up a delicious drama with all the ingredients of a bestseller—seduction, vindication, and lots of scandal."

—Brenda L. Thomas, author of *Threesome*, *Fourplay*, and *The Velvet Rope*

"Miasha tells it like it is. Her writing style is gritty and gripping, and will keep you reading and wanting more."

—Karen E. Quinones Miller, author of *Uptown Dreams*

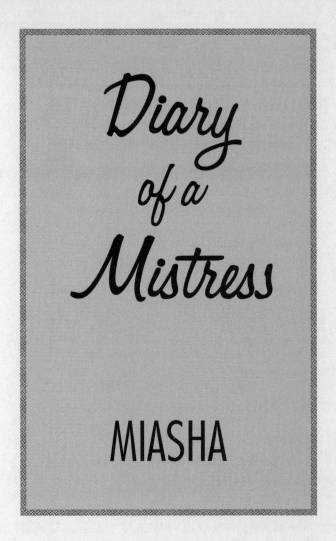

Diary of a Mistress

MIASHA

A TOUCHSTONE BOOK
Published by Simon & Schuster
New York   London   Toronto   Sydney

TOUCHSTONE
Rockefeller Center
1230 Avenue of the Americas
New York, NY 10020

This book is a work of fiction. Names, characters,
places, and incidents either are products of the
author's imagination or are used fictitiously. Any
resemblance to actual events or locales or persons,
living or dead, is entirely coincidental.

Copyright © 2006 by Meosha Coleman

TOUCHSTONE and colophon are registered trademarks
of Simon & Schuster, Inc.

For information regarding special discounts for bulk purchases,
please contact Simon & Schuster Special Sales at 1-800-456-6798
or business@simonandschuster.com.

DESIGNED BY LAUREN SIMONETTI

Manufactured in the United States of America

3   5   7   9   10   8   6   4

Library of Congress Cataloging-in-Publication Data
Miasha.
Diary of a mistress / Miasha.
p.   cm.
"A Touchstone book."
1. African American women—Fiction. 2. Mistresses—Fiction.
3. Husbands—Crimes against—Fiction. 4. Attempted murder—
Fiction. 5. Married women—Fiction. I. Title.
PS3613.I18D53   2006
813'.5—dc22   2006045029

ISBN-13: 978-0-7432-8159-1
ISBN-10:   0-7432-8159-4

This one is dedicated to you, Amir. You were
Mommy's little soldier while I wrote this book.
I wouldn't have been able to get it done
with any other newborn.

Love you,
Mommy

Chapter 1

"Hello, I'm Angie."

"Hey, Angie," a group of women said robotically, and in unison.

"I've been sleeping with married men for almost five years now, and it's getting old. I'm tired of it. I don't know if it's because I'm three days away from being thirty or if this last man I dealt with brought me to this turning point. His name was Jason. He had just got hired at my firm. He was very attractive, young, and ambitious. He definitely had his shit together. I noticed him and his wedding band all in one glance. But a wedding ring never stopped me in the past, and it wasn't going to stop me now. So I approached him. Nothing too blunt. I just introduced myself, welcomed him to the office, and made casual conversation. He was polite too, pretending to be enthused at my befriending him. But I saw right through him. He was there to do a job and nothing else. He was faithful. I gave him a couple of days, but he wouldn't budge. It was as if I didn't exist to him. A hi and good-bye was all he'd give me. At first I felt a little insulted that he didn't flirt back. But then it started to excite me. It became a game that I was determined to win. I had to break him, especially since he seemed unbreakable. I figured I would have to wait it out and get him at a vulnerable point. It was obvious to me that he and his wife were at a very happy state, probably even newlyweds. I mean, if he was over five years in, with a couple of school-age kids, he would have surely accepted my advances. But he was in love, and it was fresh. So I had to give him time. Four months went by, and one day Mr. Right came into work late—for the first time since he'd been hired. He was disoriented, not focused at all. He told everybody he wasn't feeling well. But I knew different. He was having woman problems and I was right there to solve them. I walked down the hall to his office. I knocked on his door. When he didn't answer, I let myself in. There was Mr. Right with his head down on his desk, sleeping like he hadn't all night.

"I whispered in his ear, 'Wake up, Jason, it's time for work.' "

"He must have thought I was his wife because he jumped up pleading his case.

" 'I'm sorry, baby,' he blurted out, with both pain and sincerity in his eyes.

"I remember thinking, Damn this man loved the hell out of his woman. I chuckled at his embarrassment when he realized it was just me, Angela, some lady who works at the same firm as he.

" 'Excuse me for intruding,' I said softly. 'But I thought you could use this.'

"I handed him a cup of coffee. He hesitated for a second, and then he took the cup, looked me in my eyes, and thanked me.

"I sat down in the chair opposite his desk.

" 'So, tell me,' I began. 'What are you sorry for?'

"He blushed and sipped the coffee. 'Oh, it's nothing,' he said nonchalantly.

"I smiled and said, 'Oh, it's something. It may just be nothing you want to tell me.'

"There was a brief silence.

" 'Oh, what the hell,' he said. 'I could use a woman's perspective anyway.' I finally broke the man," I told the group of women whose eyes were glued on me.

"He then began to explain to me what happened.

" 'I ran into my ex-fiancée on my way home from work yesterday. She was waiting for a bus in the rain, and she had no umbrella. Just a little plastic bag to keep her hair dry. Of course I felt bad for her, and so I offered to take her home. I made one quick stop at the cleaners, and when I got back in my car, my ex-fiancée told me that I was going to get in trouble. So I was like, What are you talking about? What makes you think that? She told me that while I was in the cleaners picking up my clothes, my wife's sister pulled up beside my car. Apparently, she cursed my ex-fiancée out and told her that she was going to tell her sister. So I get home, and my wife is all down my throat talking about, why did you have your ex-fiancée in your car, and if you were just being nice and taking her home, why the hell were you around the corner from our house when she lives on the other side of the city!'

" 'So why did you have her on the opposite side of town from where she lived if you were just taking her home? I mean, why didn't you just take her home first?' I asked him.

" 'I wanted to catch the cleaners before they closed,' Jason whined to me.

" 'Okay, that makes sense. Did you explain that to her?' I asked.

" 'Yeah, but convincing her that it's the truth was the hard part,' he said.

"This is when I decided to go in for the kill.

" 'Why doesn't your wife trust you?' I asked.

"Just like a fool in love, he rushed to his wife's defense. 'She does trust me.'

" 'Not just you, Jason, a good woman should trust your judgments as well.'

"He sat quietly for a second, going over in his head what I had said. He sipped his coffee and set the cup down on his desk. He leaned back in his chair and contemplated. Then he popped the question.

" 'Since you know so much about being a good woman, why aren't you married?'

" 'Because I also know so much about being a bad man,' I replied with a seductive grin.

"The conversation took off from there, and before long I was meeting Mr. Right in the parking lot after hours. Now, I was used to sleeping with married men, so I felt no type of way about it. But when he told me we couldn't see each other anymore because his wife had miscarried stressing over me—the other woman—I felt guilty. And it was a type of guilt—"

"YOU BITCH!" one of the women cut me off as she leaped toward me in rage.

I tried to get out of my chair and run, but it all happened so fast, I found myself paralyzed. The woman knocked my chair over with me still sitting in it. She hunched over me, her knees pressed against my chest. Her eyes were full of anger and hate. I was disoriented, struggling to move, when the woman pulled a blade from her pocket and slit my throat. I couldn't feel my own pain, but I definitely felt hers. She was Jason's wife.

Beep! Beep! Beep!

Angela jumped up out of her sleep, grabbed her butcher knife from beneath her pillow with one hand, and banged her alarm clock to death with the other. She was breathing heavily, and in a panic she began rubbing her neck checking for a cut. Looking around the room, she realized she had been dreaming. She put the knife back in its place and took a sip of the water that sat on the nightstand beside her bed. She looked at the clock. It was nine thirty.

Today was the day. She drank the last of the water, got out of bed and into some sweatpants, then took her daily four-mile jog around her apartment complex. When she got back in, she showered, ate some breakfast, and waited for the phone call. Maybe the dream was a sign to call everything off. But she had taken the day off for this, so that was not an option. Angela was anxious. She had planned everything to a T: from what she would wear to every word she would say, even the restaurant where they would meet for lunch. She knew this was her final chance to convince Carlos of their love for each other. If she waited any longer, he would slip through her fingers, especially if he went on that trip with Monica next week. This was her last shot to get him to leave his family and be with her. She was ready. The only thing she was waiting on was the phone call from Carlos. But it never came.

"What the hell?" Angela mumbled to herself as she paced her one-bedroom luxury apartment. "It's going on three o'clock."

Angela contemplated calling Carlos's cell phone, despite the fact that he had asked her not to unless he gave her direct instructions to do so. But she had expected to hear from him hours ago. Her patience was wearing thin. All the possible reasons why he hadn't called her yet ran through her head. Did he have an accident? Is he sick? Or worse, did his ass back out of our agreement, she thought. She finally broke and picked up the phone to call him.

"The number you have dialed has been disconnected at the subscriber's request."

"That bastard!" Angela shouted.

She was sick and tired of playing games with Carlos. For the whole three years of knowing him, it had been one game of cat and mouse after the other. But this was it, Angela thought. She wanted Carlos badly, and she wanted him to herself. She knew it wasn't likely for a married man to leave his wife for another woman. But she thought she was the exception. She was sure she could make Carlos do just that. All she felt she needed was a little more time.

"Mm, Carlos," Monica sighed as she rolled over on her side of the bed. "It's been a while since we went at it like that."

"I know, with the kids here all the time, it's hard," Carlos explained.

"Well, I'll be sending them to my mother's more often for a treat like this," Monica said with excitement.

The two giggled and smothered each other's body with their arms. They rolled around in their moist passion until they fell asleep in each other's bliss.

After a brief nap, Carlos woke up to the smell of cooking food. He turned over and realized his wife was not beside him. Getting out of the bed, he walked downstairs wearing nothing but a pair of boxer shorts.

"Hey, honey," Carlos said as he kissed his wife on the cheek.

Monica was standing at the kitchen sink breaking fresh collard greens with her bare hands.

"Umm, something smells good," Carlos said, taking a deep breath.

"There's salmon in the oven," Monica said, smiling.

"My favorite dish? I laid it on you then, huh?" Carlos jokingly suggested as he hugged his wife from behind.

"Go get in the shower. You smell like sex," Monica teased, bypassing Carlos's comment.

Carlos did as he was told. By the time he finished washing up and throwing on some clothes, dinner was done. The pair sat out on their deck to enjoy the delicious meal. They talked and laughed about their relationship over the years, going back as far as college. Carlos and Monica had been married for almost ten years. They first met in college. Carlos was going into his junior year and was giving a tour of the campus one summer, and Monica just happened to be in his group.

Monica was going to be a freshman that fall, and of the other female freshmen, she was among the top ten in the looks and style department. She had long jet-black hair that she tied up in a ponytail, trimmed bangs that just covered her thick, neatly arched eyebrows and accented her almond-shaped eyes. Her golden complexion resembled a perfect tan. All the latest fashions covered her shapely physique, and she was smothered in gold. She was a daddy's girl and an only child, so she was spoiled rotten. The upperclassmen were likely to be all over her. They liked what they called fresh meat. They figured new girls were naïve and vulnerable because they didn't know the guys' reputations yet, and Carlos was no different. He had taken the tour-guide position in the first place so he would have first dibs. He was a ladies' man who enjoyed flirting with all the pretty faces, and he particularly liked being able to try his hand with them before all the other guys could.

"Maybe later I can give you a tour of the dorms," Carlos said to Monica, a boyish grin on his face.

Monica looked at Carlos like he was crazy, and said, "I'll pass."

Carlos was caught off guard. He wasn't used to a response like that. His six-foot-tall, athletic build; light, soft skin; and curly hair usually got him yeses from girls right off the bat.

"What's wrong? Did I offend you?" Carlos asked, correctly reading Monica's attitude.

"What would I need a tour of the dorms for?" Monica responded.

Figuring he wasn't dealing with a ditsy cute girl, Carlos thought up a quick reply, " 'Cause if you see them, you can know which one to pick. See, they usually assign freshmen randomly, but if you know which dorm you want they'll let you choose. I'm tryna hook you up."

Monica blushed, and said, "Oh," still carrying an attitude. She was so used to guys coming at her, she kept her guard up at all times.

"See, you thought I was bein' nasty. What's on ya mind?" Carlos joked.

Monica smiled and playfully hit Carlos on his arm. It was then and there that she felt some type of chemistry between the two of them. She knew that the story about showing her the dorms was game, but she respected the fact that he had made something up. Guys like Carlos, who could probably get any girl he looked at, didn't make excuses. They saw somebody they wanted, made their advance, and if that girl wasn't with it, they said to hell with her and moved on to the next one. But Carlos was different, at least on that day, and he won her heart.

Four years went by, and they found themselves saying "I do," followed by twin sons five years after that. Carlos and Monica were inseparable. They had the type of relationship that other couples only dreamed of. It was like a fairy tale with an everlasting happy ending.

Their sons, Carlos Jr. and Christopher, looked like a perfect blend of the two of them. They both had Carlos's big cocoa brown eyes and light, smooth, buttermilk-like skin; and their mother's dark, thick hair covered their heads and formed their eyebrows. They were an adorable pair of five-year-olds, and all together they were a beautiful family.

The sun was now on its way down and the wind blew a comfortable breeze. Monica and Carlos needed that day. Between her teaching preschoolers at a summer program, his teaching workout courses at a university, and all of their spare time devoted to the twins, they hadn't spent any quality time together in a while.

It had grown dark by the time Monica and Carlos went to pick up their boys from Monica's mother. As Monica turned the key in her mother's door, a sense of excitement came over both her and Carlos. This was the first time they had spent the day without their children in a long time.

"Daddy's here," Carlos sang immediately after entering his mother-in-law's house.

"Dad-dy!" his sons squealed as they paused the video game they had been playing and ran into their father's arms. Monica stood to the side smiling as she watched her husband hug the boys.

After soaking in all the love from his sons, Carlos stepped back and looked them over. "Let me look at you two. Which one of you grew taller since yesterday?" he asked.

"I did! I did!" they both shouted, each one trying to be louder than the other.

Carlos laughed and rubbed both their heads. "Go give your mother a hug and a kiss," he said.

He then walked over to Monica's mother, who had been sitting on the sofa observing her daughter's family with delight.

"And for the second most beautiful woman in the world," Carlos said as he kissed his mother-in-law on her cheek.

Carlos was an excellent husband and father. He was

charming, respectful, committed, and good-looking. Monica took a minute to count her blessings.

The big round clock that hung in Angela's living room right above her fireplace said two o'clock. Angela was on her couch wrapped in a chenille throw, still wearing the clothes from the previous morning. An infomercial was playing on the TV. She picked up the cordless phone from the floor and checked the caller ID. Nothing. Carlos hadn't even bothered to call her. She had expected a call early in the afternoon. Now here it was two o'clock in the morning. She had taken off work for him, she thought. She was furious. She dialed the number for his home office.

"Hello," Carlos whispered, noticing Angela's name in his caller ID box. "I thought I told you not to call me past a certain time." Carlos sounded frustrated.

Angela's stomach tied up in knots. She couldn't believe Carlos's tone. "Carlos, we had a deal!"

"I know, I know, but my wife surprised me with a day off together," Carlos explained.

"But you promised! For years, you've been promising!" Angela whined.

"I don't know what you're talking about, Angela," Carlos said helplessly.

Tears began to well up in Angela's eyes.

"I'm talking about *us*. You and me, Carlos. What's going to happen to us? That's what we were supposed to discuss today, remember?"

"Listen, I have to go, and there is no us. I'm sorry," Carlos said, right before he hung up on her.

"CARLOS! CARLOS!" Angela screamed into the phone.

When she realized he had hung up, she threw her phone across the room. She began to experience a piercing pain in her stomach. She paced her apartment until she got tired. Then she balled up in a corner and wrapped her arms tightly around her knees. Her head was burning with a migraine. She was having flashbacks of all the good times she had with Carlos, the many days Carlos was the only person who kept her sane. Then, fragments of scenes from her past relationships passed through her mind: the affair her husband had, the child outside their marriage, the divorce, her pregnancy. She felt her migraine growing stronger. She needed Carlos more now than ever before. He had been the only person who could make all the pain of her past disappear. He had been her backbone, her single reason for living. And here he was telling her it was over. Just like that. No forewarning, no remorse, nothing. Everything she'd been through with him, everything he'd done for her were just distant memories. And now he would go on to be happy with his wife and children and leave Angela out on her own with nobody. She couldn't handle it. She was devastated. Walking into her bathroom, she opened the medicine cabinet and retrieved a bottle of Vicodin painkillers. She was going to put a stop to this headache. She was going to put a stop to everything.

Chapter 2

Thump! Thump! Thump!
   Thump! Thump! Thump!

"Angela! Angela! Open the door!" Angela's younger sister Ashley called out.

A week had gone by, and no one had heard from or seen her sister. First, Angela's housekeeper called Ashley earlier in the week asking about Angela, wanting to know how to collect her pay. Then Angela's boss called Ashley to find out why her sister hadn't been to work. Angela and Ashley were close, but they lived totally different lives so their paths didn't cross much. But anytime Ashley received phone calls about her sister's whereabouts, she immediately knew what was wrong.

"This is 911, what's your emergency?"

"I'm at my sister's apartment and she's inside but she's not answering the door. I'm afraid she might be hurt or unconscious or something," Ashley said in a panic.

"What's the location?"

"Bensalem Manor, apartment 3B," Ashley reported.

"We're sending an officer out, but in the meantime, try contacting the apartment's manager or maintenance and have them unlock the door. They should have a master key, and if you're listed as an emergency contact person for your sister, they'll let you in," the 911 operator instructed.

Ashley followed the operator's advice. She backed away from her sister's door and ran down the two flights of stairs. She rushed into the parking lot, jumped into her car, and drove to the office. After quickly reviewing Angela's file, the manager and Ashley went back to Angela's second-floor unit and let themselves in. The apartment was stuffy, and a horrible smell clogged the air. Ashley called her sister's name repeatedly, going from room to room, until she found her sister lying on the floor in her own vomit. Angela was barely conscious, murmuring, "Get me to the airport." She was too weak to move. Beside her was a half-empty bottle of Vicodin and an empty bottle of Merlot.

The ambulance arrived shortly thereafter. After gathering brief information about Angela from Ashley and the apartment's manager, the EMT workers put Angela on a stretcher. Ashley walked behind, watching her sister closely, as the EMTs carried Angela out of the building. The sight of her sister's unstable mental state saddened Ashley. She got in her car and followed the emergency response unit to Frankford Hospital.

As is typical for late August, the air was humid. The sun burst through the early noon clouds with power. The Philadelphia International Airport was the last place Monica thought she would end up, but when her husband pleaded with her to leave all the household chores alone and meet him there for lunch, she couldn't resist.

"Now, park the car and meet me at Terminal D. Follow the signs to Delta Airlines," Carlos instructed his wife over his cell phone.

"Okay," Monica said. "This better be a good lunch. Do you know what all I could have gotten done at the house on my day off?"

"Yeah, yeah, yeah. Just park the car and meet me over here. I never heard a woman complain so much about getting a break," Carlos teased.

"I'm parking now. I'll see you in a sec."

"Hurry up," Carlos said, then ended the call.

He was standing on the pavement near curbside check-in when his wife crept up beside him.

"You're right on time," Carlos said as he greeted Monica with a kiss on the lips.

Suspiciously, she shied away from the kiss, unsure just what her husband was up to. Monica noticed he couldn't stop smiling. He was even glowing. But before she could say a word, he led her into the airport. People were everywhere, mostly returning home from their summer vacations.

"This way," Carlos said as he led his wife through the crowds of passengers. Monica held on to Carlos's hand as he briskly weaved through the swarms of people.

"Why are you walking so fast? Are we late for a reservation? And what restaurant in the airport requires reservations anyway? Where are you taking me? Carlos, where are we going? We're not boarding any flights, are we?" she rambled on as she noticed they were heading toward the gates.

"Woman, please, shut your mouth. Just follow me. You'll see where we're going when we get there," Carlos said as he pulled two boarding passes from his denim shorts pocket and handed them to the airline employee at the gate.

The tall slender woman glanced at the boarding passes and then at the two passports that were with them. She looked up at Carlos and Monica, then gave them their passports and their portions of their boarding passes. Smiling, she said, "Enjoy your flight," and extended her arm in the direction of the aircraft.

Carlos and Monica walked down the hall to board their flight. Monica was still confused, expecting that at any minute Carlos would say, "Sike," and turn back around. But he never did. Instead, they took their seats on the plane. And not just any seats either; they were in first class.

"Oh my God, Carlos! You're lying! This is a setup! What about my clothes? What about the kids? Who's going to pick them up from camp? What about the house? How long are we going to be gone for?" Monica's excitement turned into panic as she questioned Carlos's head off.

"Don't worry, don't worry," Carlos said. "I took care of everything. Your mom has the boys. They didn't go to camp today. And your clothes are in your luggage under the plane. And Mrs. Janice agreed to keep an eye on the house. She's going to get the mail and everything," Carlos said nonchalantly.

"You're crazy," Monica said joyously as she playfully hit her husband on the arm. "I don't believe you. You planned all this by yourself? Um, um, um, I knew you had something up your sleeve, but I did not think it was anything like this. Oh my God. You got me good. I was wondering why you wanted to eat all the way at the airport, and I kept asking myself what decent restaurants were at the airport." Monica babbled on and on, excited and surprised at the same time. She continued, "Wait until I tell Rita. If she knew about this and didn't tell me, I am going to kick her behind! She's supposed to be my best friend. She can't keep something this big from me! I hope she helped you pack my clothes. Matter of fact, what clothes did you pack? I hope you didn't pack just anything. Please tell me you got Rita's approval first," Monica rambled, unable to control herself.

Carlos just kissed his wife on the lips and told her to relax. He leaned his head back and closed his eyes, pleased with how he'd managed to pull the whole thing off.

Ashley was in the waiting room for close to an hour before a doctor came out to talk to her about Angela.

"Williams?" The short Asian man approached Ashley. "I'm Dr. Wayne."

"Well, how is she?" Ashley asked.

"She's coming along. Let me ask you something, Ms. Williams, has your sister been depressed lately?" the doctor questioned.

"I'm really not sure, Doctor," Ashley said.

"Well, we've determined that Angela tried to commit suicide," the doctor explained.

Ashley shook her head, and said, "Well, I haven't been in touch with my sister for a while, but this used to happen often, like every six months after her divorce. I thought maybe she was over it since she hasn't had an episode in about three years."

"Well, I'm sorry to say it has happened again," the doctor said.

"So, I guess you'll be admitting her to Taylor's?" Ashley asked, already sure the answer was yes.

The doctor nodded, and replied, "Yes, she's being 302'd. I'm assuming you know the procedure?"

"Yeah, I'll sign the papers," Ashley said, and followed the doctor to an information desk down the hall from the waiting room.

"Good afternoon, passengers. We were due to arrive at Miami International Airport at approximately two forty-five this afternoon. But with great weather and light air traffic, it looks like we'll be landing ahead of schedule. The temperature in Miami is ninety-four degrees. I hope you have enjoyed your flight with us, and thank you for choosing Delta."

Monica opened her eyes from her catnap and looked out the window. The layers of clouds thinned out, and she was beginning to see land. She was growing more excited by the minute. Carlos was sound asleep beside her. She couldn't help but stare at him, silently appreciating him. Throughout their entire marriage, this was the best thing he had ever done for her. This topped everything, and she didn't know how to thank him for it.

"Carlos, Carlos," Monica whispered in her husband's ear. "Put your seat up; we're getting ready to land."

Carlos sat up and looked around. When he noticed people were putting their tray tables back in their upright positions, he quickly did the same. Monica was like a little kid going to Disney World. Carlos basked in her excitement.

"I still don't believe this," Monica said, giddily holding on to Carlos's arm as they exited the plane.

Carlos just smiled and said, "This is just the beginning."

He dug through his shorts pocket and pulled out his cell phone. He handed it to Monica.

"Call your mom and tell her we arrived safely," Carlos instructed his wife.

Monica dialed the numbers, still amused. Meanwhile, Carlos led them to baggage claim.

"Mom!" Monica shouted through the phone.

"Yes," Monica's mother sang.

"We're here. We're in Miami," Monica said.

"Oh, okay—"

"And I don't believe you! You knew about this and didn't tell me," Monica said excitedly.

"It was a surprise, and Carlos worked so hard to pull it off. I wasn't going to mess it up for him," Monica's mother explained. "You just go ahead and have fun. This is a much-needed vacation for you two."

"I know. Let me just yell at the boys for a second and then you won't be hearing another word from me," Monica said.

"Hold on."

"Mom-my," Christopher screeched.

"Hey, Mom!" Carlos Jr. spoke.

"Hi, boys, Mommy misses you two already," Monica sighed.

"We miss you too," her sons said in unison.

"Well, you two be good for Grandma, okay? And Mommy and Daddy will see you when we get back. Don't eat too many sweets, and make sure you go to bed on time, you hear me?" Monica told her sons, assuming they would try to take advantage of her mother.

"Okay, Mommy," the boys agreed.

"All right, that's enough." Monica's mother had taken back the phone. "Go enjoy your trip. I have everything under control here."

"All right, Mom. Thank you. I love you, and tell Chris and C.J. I love them too." Monica clicked off the phone.

"You ready?" Carlos asked Monica.

"Yes, I am, big daddy," Monica teased, still wearing her timeless smile.

Monica followed Carlos as he pushed a cart with their luggage toward the exit doors.

"Honey, look!" Monica said, pointing to a man dressed in a suit holding a sign that read: CARLOS AND MONICA VASQUEZ. Carlos approached the man unenthused. Monica, on the other hand, seemed like she had gotten a second wind, and her excitement started all over again.

"Oh my God," Monica said, holding her hand over her mouth. "No, you didn't!" She stared at the black stretch Porsche that the driver led them to.

"Madam," the driver said, as he opened the door and helped Monica inside. Carlos gave the driver a folded fifty-dollar bill as he slid in next to his wife. The driver put their luggage in the trunk and proceeded to whisk them away from the busy Miami airport.

"This is too much," Monica said, rubbing the leather seats.

"You like it?" Carlos asked. He appeared a bit amazed himself. This was the first time he had sat in something so classy. He and Monica were touching everything.

"Look, champagne!" Monica said.

"I know and look up at the ceiling, it's mirrored," Carlos pointed out.

"Um, look at this floor. It's so soft and cozy," Monica said.

The two of them went back and forth pointing out things in the Porsche. They turned knobs, pushed buttons, and eventually helped themselves to two glasses of champagne. The ride was longer than Monica expected, having assumed they would be staying in a hotel in Miami. It wasn't long before she was fast asleep.

"Sir, madam, we have arrived," the driver said as he brought the vehicle to a halt.

"Sweetheart," Carlos whispered. "We're here."

Monica sat up and peered out the small windows.

"What? Where are we?" she asked, astonished.

"Welcome to Marco Island, madam," the driver said as he escorted Monica out of the car.

Monica was at a lost for words. She looked around and could not believe her eyes. A line of beautiful big homes stretched down the beach. It looked like something from a Hollywood film.

"This isn't Miami!" Monica squealed.

"Far from it, baby. Happy tenth anniversary," Carlos said with a grin.

Monica hopped into Carlos's arms and squeezed him tight. Tears came to her eyes. She was overjoyed. They hugged for a while outside their villa, soaking in the beauty of it all. Monica fell in love with her husband all over again. It was magical.

"I'll bring your luggage inside, sir. You and your lovely wife enjoy the island," the driver said as he gave Carlos the key to the villa.

Carlos and Monica walked up the few steps and let themselves in through the home's double doors.

"Oh my God," Monica said for the one-millionth time. "This is absolutely gorgeous," she continued.

"You haven't seen anything yet," Carlos said with excitement. "This is just the foyer."

"But look at it. Look at the ceiling," Monica said.

"Yeah, it's cathedral," Carlos noted.

"Look at that chandelier," Monica continued.

"The chandelier? Wait 'til you see the pool," Carlos said, and he grabbed his wife's hand to lead her to the back of the house.

"Oh, look at these floors, and that kitchen. Oh, that fireplace is beautiful. Oh my God, look at this deck." Monica was commenting on everything she passed on her way to the pool.

"Ah!" Monica screamed, holding her hands to her mouth. "This is hot, baby!"

The pool was heart-shaped. It was filled with the prettiest blue-green water Monica had ever seen. Adjacent to it was a smaller heart that was filled with bubbling water. A couple of palm trees swayed gently in the wind. A patio table and two chairs were placed a short distance from the pool. The whole area was enclosed by black iron gates. In the distance other beautiful homes were set against the open sky. Monica stood stiff as she took in the scenery. She had been spoiled as a child and had gotten everything she saw and asked for. But never had she seen anything like this.

"It's nice, isn't it," Carlos asked as he crept up behind his wife and wrapped his arms around her.

"Carlos, nice? This is amazing," she exclaimed.

Carlos and Monica stood there in the middle of the luxurious setting, paralyzed by the beauty around them.

Angela entered the Taylor's Institution for Behavioral Health accompanied by two emergency medical technicians. She was taken to the admissions room, where she was met by a psychiatric technician. After answering a few questions, Angela was introduced to a nurse who did a quick examination. When she was finally settled into a room, a counselor bought her some dinner. The next day she was scheduled to see a psychiatrist, who would determine whether or not she needed to be put on medication. It was all routine for Angela, who had traveled this road several times in the past. She just went with the flow, wanting to get the process over with as quickly and smoothly as possible. She wasn't going to give anybody any trouble like she had in the past. They weren't going to have to restrain her this time around. She knew the fastest way out of the institution was through displaying cooperation and stability, so she strictly followed all the rules. Her plan was to be discharged as soon as possible so that she could get back to living her normal life, and to her that meant being with Carlos.

The next day a staff member woke Angela and told her that she was scheduled to meet with the psychiatrist that morning. Angela washed, got dressed, and was escorted into the doctor's office at the end of the hall.

"Good morning, Ms. Williams. I'm Dr. Whitaker," the forty-something dark-skinned woman greeted Angela.

"Good morning," Angela responded casually.

The doctor pulled a folder from beneath a couple of books on her desk and opened it. She picked up a pair of reading glasses that sat nearby and placed them over her eyes.

"I've noticed your evaluations so far have been good. You slept through the night without any incident. You didn't demand anything that could have been harmful to you. That's a plus. If you keep it up, maintain your behavior, and follow our directions, you could be discharged after the court hearing," the doctor told Angela as she jotted something down in the folder.

"That's my goal, Dr. Whitaker," Angela said.

"Oh, it is, is it?" Dr. Whitaker probed as she stopped writing and looked up at Angela.

"Yes, I don't intend on being here any longer than a week," Angela said with confidence.

"So what's your goal once you do get out of here?" Dr. Whitaker asked, removing her glasses.

"Well," Angela began, "first, I plan to go back to work."

"And what kind of work do you do?" Dr. Whitaker asked.

"I was an executive VP at a major marketing firm."

Dr. Whitaker's face wrinkled. "How on earth did you end up here?"

Angela blushed. "You know, I've asked myself that repeatedly, Doctor, and I never come to a real answer. All I know is I let a man get the best of me, once again."

"A husband?" Dr. Whitaker said.

"Yes, just not *my* husband," Angela responded.

"Let me guess, you were waiting on the sidelines for him to get a divorce and when it never happened you snapped?" Dr. Whitaker said.

"I wish that were all," Angela began. "It got to the point where he was dictating my life. I would stop whatever I was doing and rush home just to be by the phone when he called, and when he didn't call, I blamed myself. I would think I wasn't fast enough and missed the call or something. Then I wound up getting a phone with caller ID," Angela explained.

"What brought you to your breaking point?" Dr. Whitaker probed.

"To be quite honest, I was far gone before he told me he couldn't see me anymore. You see, I was on the other side of the fence with my own husband, and that's what started all this craziness." Angela grew upset as she thought about her ex-husband. Tears fell slowly down her cheeks. She wasn't sure if she was ready to deal with the issue of Carlos and her mental state.

Dr. Whitaker handed her a tissue and told her, "We don't have to go any further, today."

"Thank you, because I don't want to talk about it. It just might be good for me to leave it alone," Angela said as she sniffed and held back her tears. "Besides, I'm concentrating on me now, on how I'm going to get out of here."

Dr. Whitaker smiled. She put her glasses back on and made another notation on Angela's chart.

"Well, that's perfectly fine, but let me offer a suggestion," Dr. Whitaker said. "Start a journal, a diary, something in which you can write all of your feelings down. This way you're getting all of the emotions and pain out of your system. You can release without actually talking." Dr. Whitaker dug in her desk drawer and pulled out a diary, then handed it to Angela and said, "Try it."

Angela took the diary and dabbed her eyes again with the tissue. "Thank you," Angela said softly.

"Now, I'm going to prescribe a small dosage of Zoloft just to balance you out. But, Ms. Williams, you have nothing to be ashamed of," Dr. Whitaker said as she looked Angela in her eyes. "There are plenty of normal, everyday people who end up in places like this. We get so caught up in living normal that we don't realize what things in our lives are making us abnormal, and it's not until we snap one day that we realize we're only human and there's only so much we can take before we lose it. That's why it's important to rid ourselves of all the pain, all the negative feelings, all the bad vibes that we may get from people. It's important to get it off of us and transfer it someplace else. We can't bear the burden of other people's ill intentions. So you use that diary. Write in it all the time. Get all of the feelings you store inside of you out and put them on those pages. Slowly but surely, you'll feel renewed."

Chapter 3

"Rise and shine," Carlos said softly as he entered the bedroom where his wife was still asleep.

It was Carlos and Monica's fifth day on Marco Island together, and Carlos had decided to surprise his wife with breakfast in bed. He was carrying a tray of food toward the king-size bed where Monica was curled up.

"Um," Monica sighed as she opened her eyes and stretched. "Aww, honey," she mumbled. "You shouldn't have."

"You deserve it," Carlos said as he placed the tray on his wife's lap. "It's all your favorites: a cheese omelet, smoked turkey sausage, a side of home fries with onions, and a bowl of ambrosia," Carlos listed.

"And my cappuccino?" Monica asked. "You're such a sweetheart," she added.

She sat up in the bed and scanned the suite. She looked over at the bathroom, which had a glass door so that she could see straight through to the marble Jacuzzi tub. On the other side of the suite, French doors led out to the balcony, which overlooked the sandy beach. In front of her was a stacked-stone fireplace. Finally, she raised her head toward the ceiling, which seemed to go on forever, reaching far up to a skylight. She wanted to etch the beauty of the house in her memory, hoping never to forget a single thing.

"This is what I'm talking about," Monica said as she cut a piece of her omelet. "Um, um, um, I must be a hell of a wife to get all of this," she joked, placing the bite in her mouth.

"You are," Carlos said with a straight face. He stretched out across the foot of the bed.

"And you are one hell of a husband," Monica said, tickling Carlos's arm with her toes.

Carlos smiled at her. It was obvious he loved making his wife happy. It seemed as if he felt the most joy when she was pleased at something he'd said or done. Monica relished the thought of how deeply in love Carlos was with her and felt blessed to have a husband like him.

"I'm still amazed at all of this. I mean, I can actually hear the waves crashing against the shore. This is my life. My husband did all of this for me." Monica spoke with a humble smile.

"You never saw this coming, did you?" Carlos asked, still wanting his credit for planning such a thorough surprise.

"Never. Not at all. Not even when you begged me to meet you at the airport for lunch," Monica responded, sipping her cappuccino.

"Well, I've been planning this since last year," he said. "I spoke to your boss and asked her to put you down for a vacation this week. I even made sure to schedule the trip a week before the actual anniversary date so that you wouldn't suspect anything," he bragged.

"Well, I must say, all of that planning has paid off, because you definitely caught me by surprise. This was the most well-put-together plan I've ever heard of. I mean, this has to be up there with God's creation of earth," Monica joked, stroking her husband's ego.

"Ten years. Can you believe it's been that long?" Carlos asked, reflecting on their marriage.

"I know, it seems like yesterday," Monica said in the same reflective mode.

"I love you, Monica. I do, and I am going to love sharing ten more years with you," Carlos said, with the type of sincerity Monica knew all too well from her husband.

"I love you too," she responded, "and this has been a wonderful vacation so far," she added, leaning forward and kissing her husband on his lips.

"Angela, it's time to take your meds!" shouted a short, heavyset, brown-skinned nurse.

Angela walked out of her room and slowly proceeded beneath the bright fluorescent lights down the wide hallway. Her fellow mental-health patients were scattered about in the sitting area playing cards, watching television, and talking with one another. She didn't say anything to any of them as she walked to the nurse's station to accept her medication. She had been institutionalized for five days thus far. She'd spent her first day and night on suicide watch, her second day being evaluated by a psychiatrist, and the remaining three days in her room writing.

"Thank you, Vanessa," Angela said as she gulped down the water and the two tiny pills.

"Thank you, Angela," the nurse responded. "You're behaving so well this time. Keep it up, and you may just be outta here after seeing the judge on Monday."

"That's my plan," Angela said with a grin.

"Oh, yeah? Is that why you stay in your room? You don't want any run-ins with anybody, huh?" Vanessa quizzed.

"Exactly," Angela responded. "The last time I was in here, the judge only committed me to thirty days, and that turned into ten months, all because of fighting with these people. I'd rather stay in my room all day and avoid that drama and be able to walk out those doors immediately after court than mingle with fake friends and risk having to be in here for a whole year."

"I hear that," Vanessa said. "What do you do in there all day, though? I know you gotta get bored."

"I exercise, read, and mostly I write."

"What, poetry or something?"

"No. A diary."

"Oh, yeah? I used to keep a diary back when I was in college," Vanessa said.

"Well, Dr. Whitaker suggested I start one. She said since I have a hard time talking about my feelings, it might be best to write them down in a diary. That way I'm getting things off my chest. You know . . . out of my system," Angela explained.

"Yeah, that makes sense. Well, go ahead. I won't keep you. If you need anything, just give me a holler," Vanessa said as she scribbled something down on a sheet of paper.

Angela began to walk back down the hall toward her room. She stopped midway and turned back toward

Vanessa. "Oh, Vanessa! I'm going to need you to mail something for me." Angela spoke as if the thought had just popped in her head.

"Oh, okay," Vanessa said, "I'll take it with me when my shift ends."

"Thanks," Angela replied, then continued back to her room. Once inside the small square room, Angela retrieved her diary from under the twin mattress. She turned to an empty page in the back of the book and started writing. She had to hurry if she was going to finish it by the end of Vanessa's shift at three that afternoon. As she was writing, she was thinking. It seemed like forever since she last heard Carlos's voice—a lonely, hectic time. She wanted Carlos more than anything, and she knew that if she only had the opportunity to see him again, she would be able to win him over. The relationship had started as a casual one. She had a companion without the hassles of a commitment. But it quickly turned into something serious. She had begun to arrange her life around Carlos, missing work and signing up for all his classes no matter how they conflicted with her schedule. She fully expected that one day the two of them would share an exclusive relationship. All of her dreams were to come true with him. They would get married and have children, and he would be the one to finally rescue her from her past, bringing an end to her fear of being alone for the rest of her life. Carlos made her feel comfortable and secure about herself. He made her forget all of the shame, embarrassment, and pain that her ex-husband and other men had caused her. Carlos became her drug, allowing her to escape her reality. Now she was over the deep end for him, ready and willing to do anything to get him and keep him. She thought she was woman enough to make him leave his wife, but it seemed as if she would need to cause havoc between him and his wife. And she had just the plan.

It was a beautiful Monday in September. The leaves on the trees were that dusty end-of-summer green. The sun was shining bright, giving just enough heat to offset the breeze. One couldn't ask for a better Labor Day. It was also the day that Monica and Carlos got married exactly ten years ago. The happy couple had just returned from their anniversary vacation. They picked up their car from the airport parking lot, packed their bags in its trunk, and drove off. They missed the sandy Floridian beach, but they were happy to be home and eager to see their boys.

Carlos dropped Monica and their luggage off at their home in northeast Philadelphia's Rhawnhurst section. He was going to pick up their sons from his mother-in-law's while Monica got a head start on the unpacking.

"Hey, Monica. Hey, Carlos!" an older female yelled as she waved to her neighbors.

Carlos beeped his horn and waved at the woman as he backed out of his driveway.

"Hi, Mrs. Janice," Monica called to the woman.

"I have your mail," Mrs. Janice said, motioning for Monica to come over.

Monica started across the lawn to the driveway that separated their houses. Mrs. Janice met her halfway, carrying a bundle of mail in one hand and a package in the other.

"Thank you so much, Mrs. Janice," Monica said.

"No problem, love. How was the trip? Were you surprised?" Mrs. Janice asked with a big grin.

"Yeah, he got me good. But it was beautiful. We had a good time," Monica told her, blushing.

"That's good. Listen, I'm cooking on the grill and having some people over. You, Carlos, and the kids are welcome if you like. My daughter's coming down from Connecticut. She's bringing my grandbabies," Mrs. Janice said, smiling.

"Oh, that sounds nice," Monica said. "But I have so much unpacking to do, I think I'll have to pass. Thanks for the invitation, though."

"No problem, but if you want you can send the boys over. I'll keep an eye on them while you and Carlos do what y'all have to do," Mrs. Janice offered, then started to make her way back over to her house.

"Okay, thanks, Mrs. Janice," Monica said, and headed to her own front door.

"Oh, and Monica, I'll send you two over a plate!" Mrs. Janice yelled.

Monica smiled and thanked Mrs. Janice once more before retreating into her house. She walked past the luggage that cluttered her living room and jogged up the steps. Plopping down on her bed, she started rummaging through the handful of mail she had gotten from Mrs. Janice.

"Oh, it feels good to be home," she said under her breath. "Junk, junk, bills," Monica mumbled as she skimmed through envelopes and circulars.

Monica came across the white box that had "Priority Mail" marked on the front. Her name and address were written in a fancy cursive on the mailing label. The return address was illegible. She wasn't expecting anything from anybody, and she hadn't ordered anything online, so she had no idea what it was. She then immediately thought it was yet another surprise from Carlos, and the expression on her face went from confused to excited.

"This man doesn't know when to quit," she said to herself as she shook the box gently. It had a little weight to it, but nothing rattled around inside. Was it jewelry? Her favorite perfume?

She got up off the bed and walked over to a chest that stood against the wall. She pulled a pair of scissors from the top drawer, sat back on the bed, and started poking the creases of the box with the scissors. When she opened the box and saw one of Carlos's sweatshirts folded neatly inside, her smile grew bigger. But confusion returned when beneath the shirt, still inside the box, she noticed one more item. It was a diary.

Chapter 4

"Can I have my phone call before we go outside?" Angela asked the tall, thin brown-skinned girl who sat at the office window in the center of the unit.

"Your hour isn't until later this evening, Ms. Angie," the girl responded as she peered over a chart that was taped next to the telephone.

"You can give her the call now. It's okay," Vanessa butted in from inside the office.

The girl shrugged her shoulders and handed Angela the telephone through the Plexiglas window.

"Be quick though, because we're going out in ten minutes."

Angela rolled her eyes and started dialing numbers on the telephone. After a few rings her sister picked up.

"Hello," Ashley answered loudly.

Angela momentarily moved the phone away from her ear and frowned. "Goodness, you're loud," she said.

"Oh, hold on, Angie," Ashley said. "Turn that radio down some, please!"

"What, are you at a party?" Angela asked.

"My girlfriend's cookout. What's up?"

"I'm just calling to tell you my court date is tomorrow. Do you think you'll be able to make it? It's at ten."

"Oh, um, yeah. I'm glad you called, though, because I had plans for tomorrow. But I'll just cancel. Where will it be?"

"The hospital, as always," Angela said.

"Norristown State?" Ashley confirmed.

"Yeah, I'm not sure what room, but you can just—"

"Ask the guy at information," Ashley finished Angela's sentence.

"Yeah, you know what to do."

"Okay. Well, I'll see you then," Ashley said quickly.

"Well, um, I see you're busy, so I'm going to let you go," Angela said.

"All right then. I'll see you tomorrow. 'Bye."

Angela hung up the phone.

"Thanks, Vanessa," Angela said, emphasizing Vanessa's name as she walked away from the window.

The young girl smirked at her and said, "Vanessa? I'm the one who handed you the phone."

"Yeah, after *Vanessa* told you to," Angela snapped.

"Just 'cause Vanessa told me it was okay didn't mean I had to let you make your call. Technically, you would have had to wait until eight o'clock like it says on the chart, regardless what Vanessa said."

"Little girl, I will—" Angela began before Vanessa came out of the office and stood in front of her.

"Angela," Vanessa said, "remember your goal now. You're tryin' to get discharged tomorrow. Don't let nothin' get in the way of that."

Angela took a deep breath and turned her back to the

girl. She proceeded to walk down the hall toward her room.

"It's Labor Day and y'all get to go outside and enjoy the beautiful weather, eat some barbecue, and listen to some music. Don't mess that up," Vanessa added as she walked alongside Angela.

"You're right. Now you see why I stay in my room. It's like these young girls be just waitin' to take you off your square."

"I know. And you're doing the right thing by staying to yourself. Speaking of which, you filled that diary up quick. You must have had a lot on your chest. I didn't know anybody could write so fast. The last diary I kept took me two years to fill up. Who was that you had me mail it to anyway?" Vanessa finally asked.

"Oh, just a friend of mine. It's all a part of the therapeutic process, you know?" Angela said, turning the knob to her room.

"So what now? Your friend's supposed to read it?" Vanessa asked.

"I would hope so. I would hope I didn't do all that writing for nothing," Angela said, smiling before she disappeared into her room.

Dear Diary,

How did I ever get caught up in this lifestyle? Just four years ago I was a wife on my honeymoon planning the happily ever after, and now here I am taking that plan away from another woman. But am I wrong? I mean, I've been on both sides of the fence, and I must say the trade is much more fair being the mistress. Why sit at home carrying the burden of wondering, is my man fucking another woman? And even if you do trust his ass 100 percent, you still have to wonder if he's fucking another woman. Because let's face it, that is what men do. They find a good woman, somebody they proclaim to want to spend the rest of their lives with, somebody perfect enough to bear their children, and then shortly after or shortly before they marry, they find the woman they can just fuck. You know, the one with no strings attached. The one who won't ever argue with his ass because she doesn't give a damn about him. The one that won't ever nag his ass because she's getting everything she could possibly want from him. The other woman. Me now, but her then. Maybe that's what this is all about. I married my high school sweetheart. We were both eighteen and deeply in love. We were each other's soul mate until I went off to college. In the beginning it was fine. He visited the campus so much people thought he was a student. Then he got a new job, and things changed. The visits slowed up. He claimed the fifty-five miles each way was too much on his car. The next thing I knew, he was having an affair with a coworker, and they produced a child. To him he was just cheating on me. To me it was an affair. We were married shit! When a man or a woman cheats while they're married, it's called an affair, jackass. That just went to show how young and not ready for marriage he really was. He didn't consider himself to be having an af-

fair. He didn't consider the other woman his mistress. He must not have considered us married. In his underdeveloped mind we were probably still just boyfriend and girlfriend. Not to say that cheating is okay when you're just messing with somebody, but damn it, when you get married, that's supposed to be that! Listen to me blabbering on about how my husband hurt me. That was then, and this is now. I'm twenty-six years old. I've been divorced for just over a year. I have no children. I have a master's in communications. I'm very attractive, with a body guys would call perfect: 36-24-36. And I'm independent. It would be wrong for me to let all this good woman go to waste on a muthafucka that's gonna do me dirty. So what, I'm the other woman. In a relationship it's the other woman who has all the fun. Do I feel sorry for the wives of the men I deal with? Well, maybe I would if I believed that their husbands would be faithful if it weren't for me. Guys are going to sleep with another woman anyway. So it might as well be me. I might as well be the one to get the perks. Yes, there are perks to being a mistress. Gifts, money, vacations, and overall good times. You see, the mistress gets a lot of things just for her cooperation. A wife, on the other hand, is expected to stand by her man regardless of what she gets or doesn't get. All he has to do is lie and say he's financially fucked up at the moment, and she's supposed to be like, okay, baby, we'll work through this together. All the while his ass is funding my lifestyle. And that's sup-

posed to assure him that I won't blow his cover. Lil' Kim said it best, "I'ma throw shade, if I can't get paid,/ Blow you up to you girl like the Army grenade." And don't get me wrong, I'm not a money-hungry chick who listens to too much Lil' Kim shit. I'm just saying. Anyway, the question was am I wrong. The answer so far is no.

"What the hell?" Monica mumbled as she came to the end of the diary entry. Who sent me this nonsense? A woman's diary and my husband's shirt, she thought as she held the shirt in one hand and the diary in the other. This can't be what I think it is. Well, hell, I'm sure about to read and find out.

Monica put the shirt back on the bed and reopened the diary to the page where she had left off. With her brow furrowed, she reread the last couple of sentences and turned to the next entry.

Dear Diary,

The time has come for you to meet Carlos. He's fine as shit. And he's half Puerto Rican, so you know what that means—good hair. He's a personal trainer too, so you know what that means—nice-ass body. And he took a trip down the aisle, so you know what that means—he's married. He lives in the Northeast with his wife, Monica, and their twin sons, C.J. and Christopher. They would seem to be the perfect family from the outside looking in, but, according to Carlos, it's boring. He loves his sons to death and wouldn't consider being a dad boring

*but being a husband to Monica is. He tells me that
she never wants to do anything but sit on the couch
watching talk show after talk show and occasionally a home-decorating show. And as for the sex, he
told me it's like pulling teeth. He said ever since
their twins were born her sex drive been in neutral.
He said he has to push with all his might to move
it, and then when it finally does move, it rolls real
slow. I had to laugh at that analogy, although it really wasn't funny. It's fucked up how men have a
hard time understanding women's issues with hor-
mones and surgeries and shit that they don't have
to deal with. But let the shoe be on the other foot.
Let a man have problems getting up. His woman is
supposed to support him, get him some Viagra, or
use a vibrator or something. The bottom line is,
she's not supposed to use his malfunction as an excuse to mess with another man behind his back.
But a man? That's a whole different story. He's
most likely going to have an affair anyway, so if he
has a so-called good reason to do so, that's even
better—for him and his conscience.*

*Anyway, Carlos and I met at a restaurant down-
town. He was eating with a client of his, and I was
having dinner with David. I never told you about
David because he wasn't worth the pen and paper.
He was just a fling for me, especially after I found
out just how scandalous he was. You're probably
thinking shit, any man who sleeps around on his
wife is scandalous. But that's not necessarily the
case. You got some men that just can't help them-*

selves but they do it respectably and still manage to keep their wives happy. And you got some men who love their wives and are happy with their wives but who were probably ugly in their younger and broker days and didn't get many women and definitely not any pretty women. Then they get successful and attract all kinds of chicks when they pull up in a Benz. So they jump at every opportunity they missed in the past. It's almost like a once-in-a-lifetime thing for them, so they kind of go buck wild sleeping with different women. It makes them finally feel good about themselves. It makes them feel like men. Then you got other men who just don't give a fuck. They'll fuck your next-door neighbor in the five minutes it takes you to brush your teeth. That was David—the type that would go to the store for a pack of cigarettes on a Saturday afternoon and not come back until Monday morning. But some things men do you have to blame their wives for, because that chick, Sharon, would let his ass do anything under the sun, and all she would do was curse his ass out and tell him she wasn't letting him leave her. Now that was some re-tarded shit. Her theory was that he would cheat on her and disrespect her like that just so she would have a reason to leave him. And in her mind, she figured if that's what he wanted she wasn't going to give it to him. Naw, hell no, just for that she was going to stay with his trifling ass forever and make him miserable. Bullshit! He was not miserable. He was the happiest muthafucka on the planet. He could blatantly cheat on his wife over and over again, and his only consequence was that he had to stay with her. A woman like that deserves to be cheated on because she got her shit all fucked up. Needless to say, I had no remorse whatsoever for her. But I eventually had to stop messing with David. He was just too scandalous for me. I mean, I participated in some scandals with him, like when I almost got caught in his house while his wife was at work. She wasn't supposed to be home for another two hours. But this day she decided to leave work early. She probably had a feeling something was going on at her house. You know that women's intuition shit is right!

Anyway, I was upstairs in the bathroom getting myself together. The next thing I knew David was screaming, Yo! My wife is coming, you gotta bounce! Yeah, David was hood. Anyway, just as she was opening her front door, I came walking out of her house smiling. Luckily, I was quick on my toes. "You must be the lucky lady," I said to David's wife. She was looking at me confused, like she didn't know whether to start going off on me or listen to me explain why the hell she was so lucky. "I'm Ashley, an Avon representative, and I just sold your husband here a cosmetic demonstration that includes a makeover for you and four friends. He wanted to surprise you for your birthday, but he wasn't expecting you home so early." David was standing in the doorway smiling nervously. His wife started smiling too, after I fed her that lie. She thanked David and gave him a big hug and a kiss and everything. I was cracking up laughing on the inside, and even though I could have left like that without Sharon getting any suspicions about my story, I sealed the deal. I pulled my wallet from my pocketbook and took my sister Ashley's business card out. I handed it to Sharon. She smiled again and thanked me. I told the happy couple I would set up an appointment with them over the phone. Well, I really saved David's ass that time because I had my sister set up a demonstration and give Sharon and four other chicks free makeovers. I had to stop messing with David after that, though, because he expected me to take more risks like that one. He figured I could get us out of anything, like I was a genie, like I walked around with a rabbit in my hat or some shit. I had to explain to him that I was lucky only that one time, and besides his wife was hood just like him. I wasn't tryin' to walk outside one day and see my car all keyed up with my windows busted and my tires flat. Fuck that.

But back to Carlos, my week-old romance. I was going in the ladies' room, and he was coming out of the men's room. We locked eyes for a moment, and then we each went our separate ways. All through dinner I kept looking around the restaurant trying to find the man from the bathroom. Apparently, it was a mutual thing. We made eye contact again and signaled to meet back at the restrooms. I slid him my number and returned to my booth with David.

I got a phone call the next day. Carlos and I talked on the phone for hours, feeling each other out. He told me right away about his wife. I usually bypassed conversations about the wife, but I was curious this time. I asked Carlos why did he ever pursue me if he was married. He told me that he and his wife were having problems, and he was simply looking for something different. He said he was just unhappy and bored with his love life. He was looking for some excitement, and he said he and his wife would soon be divorcing.

Monica slammed the diary shut. She could not believe what she was reading. After a minute, she started laughing to herself uncontrollably. She figured somebody was playing games with her, trying to mess up her marriage. Me and my husband are absolutely happy. This jealous bitch don't know what she's talkin' about. She should have really got her facts straight before she tried to pull one on me. I have to call Rita and tell her about this shit.

"Well, hello, there. How was Marco Island? Did you fulfill all your fantasies?" Rita sang into the phone.

"Hey, Rita. I had a wonderful time. And I still got some bones to pick with you, miss. Keeping a secret like that from me. I'm shocked!"

"Believe me, it wasn't easy. I still got blisters from biting my tongue," Rita said.

"Well, anyway, I'll have to tell you about the trip later, but guess what I got in the mail?" Monica began.

"If you anything like me, bills and cheap thrills."

"Oh, but this is the best cheap thrill you gonna ever hear about."

"What?"

"Why did some chick send me one of Carlos's sweat-shirts—"

"What?" Rita butted in.

"Wait. Hold up. That's not it. Underneath the shirt was a diary," Monica continued.

"A diary?"

"Yes. At first I thought it was something from Carlos because he's been in this surprising mood lately, and it didn't have a return address on it. But I opened the diary and started reading, and it's a woman talking about messing around with people's husbands. And not only that: my husband is one of them."

"You lyin'," Rita gasped.

"Rita, I lie to you not. But the funny thing about it is she's talkin' about stuff that ain't true. Like for instance," Monica started to explain as she opened the diary, "she talks about how Carlos told her we're having problems and on the verge of divorce."

"Oh, well, there you have it. It's a prank. You know like I know, for every one happy woman there's one thousand miserable ones just waiting to take her place," Rita concluded. "I would like to know which miserable one is bold enough to send some shit to your home. She don't say her name in there anywhere?"

Monica began to scan the pages in search of the woman's identity.

Her voice was muffled as she read aloud, " 'September 20th, 2000—' "

Rita cut her off, "2000! She's talkin' about shit that happened four years ago. Oh, please."

"I know, right." Monica chuckled. "Listen to this. 'Dear Diary: Carlos and I are really hitting it off. He's a romantic. Today he met me outside of my job with a bouquet of white roses. He said it was just something small to celebrate our one-month anniversary.' "

"One-month anniversary? Is it really that serious?" Rita burst into laughter. "Like a man would really put out the time and effort to make plans for a one-month anniversary. Shit, it's hard enough to remember his yearly anniversary with his wife, let alone some month-by-month shit with some side dish! Oh, you gotta be kiddin' me. This chick is tryin' hard to piss you off, Monica. Read the rest. This shit is crackin' me up."

Monica chuckled at Rita's comments, but inside she was feeling insecure. She thought herself that the diary was made up and sent by some jealous woman, but her husband's shirt was still an unsolved mystery. She couldn't help but wonder how this unknown female got her hands on Carlos's clothing. She continued reading.

" 'He had reservations for us at a bistro in Jersey. I really enjoyed myself. It was easy for me to forget he was married. After dinner we drove to a deserted location where we just watched the stars and talked. It was very late when he dropped me off at my car, which was parked back at my job. He politely kissed me on my lips and drove off. He was a perfect gentleman. I felt bad for his wife because she was losing a good man. But some relationships just aren't meant to last.' "

"Um, um, um. What other bullshit is in that book?" Rita asked.

Monica skimmed through the pages. "Oh, here goes something from 2001," she said, feeding Rita's frenzy.

" 'December 28, 2001. Dear Diary: Last year Carlos had to spend Christmas with his family. But this year he said he would spend the holidays with me. He had a well-thought-out plan too. He told his wife he would spend the early part of the day with her and the kids and then drive down to Florida to spend some time with his mother and brother. He knew his wife would avoid any chance to visit his mom because they didn't get along with each other. As for his boys, Monica was still at the point where she didn't trust them being anywhere without her. So he knew it wouldn't seem suspicious if he took the drive alone. His wife fell for it. Shit, let that had been me. I would have checked his mileage. But anyway, he came to my apartment around six o'clock Christmas Day. I had a good meal prepared, some Cornish hens, sweet potatoes, rice and gravy, sliced ham, collard greens, and cranberry sauce. For dessert, I baked an apple pie and served it with vanilla ice cream. We ate dinner then went out for a movie in Langhorne. Once we got back to my place we finally made love.'

"Oh, no, see, now she's takin' it too far," Monica said.

"Keep readin'. This is the good part," Rita jumped in.

"Rita, how did she know about that Christmas?"

"I don't know, but let's find out. Keep readin'," Rita instigated.

" 'It's been a whole year and we've spent a lot of time together, you know, whenever his wife would go to the nursing home to see her dad, and the time she went to Texas for her family reunion, but he kept saying he wanted to wait until the time was right.' " Monica slammed the book shut. The nerve of that son of a bitch, she thought.

"Rita, I do not believe this! She knows a little too much. What if Carlos—"

"Hold up. Now, Monica, you know Carlos like the back of your hand. Don't you think you would have sensed something, had he been cheating on you all this time? Don't lose your cool so quick."

"But she knows entirely too much stuff. Like this, listen to this," Monica said, as she found a random page in the middle of the book. "It says, 'March 3, 2002. Dear Diary: Today Carlos stood me up. We were supposed to get together and go down to the casino. But his wife caught mono from one of those kids she teaches.' Remember that? How would she know that?" Monica asked.

"But plenty of people knew about that," Rita said.

"Like who? My family and close friends, and a few of his close friends, and the other teachers, of course. But that's it," Monica explained.

"Exactly!" Rita said, "It could be a number of people playing with you. I bet you it's one of them fake-ass teacher friends. Think, who would want to cause problems between you and Carlos?"

Monica ignored Rita's question. At that point she no longer believed the diary was a hoax like Rita did. Her heart began to beat faster.

"Listen to this," Monica started up again. " 'You

won't believe who I ran into down Penn's Landing today—Carlos and Monica. This was my first time seeing her. She's cute. She had on a cute outfit too. Some fitted white pants and a red-and-white halter and some red stilettos. She didn't look anything like the wholesome schoolteacher Carlos described.' I remember exactly what day she's talking about, and nobody we know saw us down there because they would have stopped and spoke," Monica concluded.

"Well, yeah, I guess so," Rita agreed. "What else does she say about that day? Maybe there's a hint in there about who she is."

Monica read on. " 'Carlos looked a little scared like I was going to play his cards in front of his wife. I wanted to real bad, especially now that he hasn't called me ever since I told him I was . . .' Oh, my God, Rita! I will *kill* that man!" Monica shouted.

"What, Monica?" Rita asked.

"This bitch was pregnant by my husband!" Monica yelled. "Rita! Wait 'til he brings his ass in here! I will kill that man! I swear to God!"

At that moment Rita started to take the diary more seriously. She could tell Monica was hurt, and as her best friend she wanted to console her. "Monica, calm down, sweetheart, you still don't know if this is true or not."

"It better not be true, Rita! Because if it is, Carlos is a dead man! How could he do something like this to me?"

"Well, where is Carlos now? You should ask him about this," Rita suggested.

"He went to Mom's to pick up the boys," Monica told her.

"Well, I'm coming to get you," Rita decided.

"For what? I wanna be right here when he gets back so I can . . . OH! I don't believe this shit!" Monica shouted, tears gathering in her eyes.

"Monica, you don't need to be there when he gets there. How you're feelin' right now, there's no tellin' what you will do when he comes through that door, and you don't want the boys to be in the middle of all that." Rita made a rational point.

Monica took into consideration what Rita was saying. Her best friend was right. C.J. and Chris didn't need to know what was going on. She thought maybe it would be best for her to go over to Rita's, at least until she calmed down some.

"All right," Monica said, letting out a sigh. "His ass is lucky I love my sons like I do, otherwise, I swear to God . . ."

Chapter 5

Rita's row home off of Cottman Avenue wasn't but ten minutes away from Monica's. But with it being Labor Day, every other street was blocked off. Rita had to take detours, turning her typically ten-minute drive into a twenty-minute one. And Monica kept her eyes glued to the diary the entire time, not even budging the couple times Rita tried to get her to look at a block party.

When they finally got to Rita's, Monica plopped into a recliner chair, tucking her feet under her behind. Her face was stained from the mixture of her tears and mascara. She was reading the diary page by page, reciting some parts of it to Rita. She was growing more and more angry with each entry, in complete and utter disbelief at the things that were being revealed about Carlos.

"You need to put that book down. You've read enough," Rita told Monica.

"Before you were tellin' me to read everything!" Monica shot at her friend.

"Yeah, but that was when it was amusing. The shit ain't funny no more. It's hurting you. And it's hurting me because I can't address the bitch who's bringin' you this drama," Rita said as she practically slammed a cup of lemonade on a wooden end table beside Monica.

"Listen to this," Monica said, turning her attention back to the diary, and disregarding Rita's speech.

Rita sat down on the sofa diagonal from Monica and rolled her eyes. She let out a sigh, but kept silent as she listened to Monica read.

" 'I'm three months pregnant with his got damn baby, and he wants me to get an abortion. When I told him I didn't believe in abortions, he told me that was my problem. He said I would end up raising the kid on my own, and he would never have anything more to do with me. I'm the stupid one, though. I should have figured if he wanted me to get rid of our baby that bad, he must have had no intentions on leaving Monica. He was trying to protect his marriage. He didn't want his wife to find out about us and definitely not a baby. I should have the damn baby anyway, and I should take his ass to court for child support and see how he likes it. His wife would really be pissed if she had to find out about her husband's affair in a courtroom. As a matter of fact, I think I'm going to do just that.' "

"All right, look. That was in '02, right? Well, if this is all true and this broad had a baby by your husband, don't you think she would have executed her plan by now? Why hasn't she taken Carlos to court? I know I would, wife or not!" Rita said, still trying to discredit the diary.

Meanwhile Monica's eyes had not lifted from the pages.

" 'October 12th, 2002. Dear Diary: Tonight was the

final straw. He knows I'm pregnant—five months at that. I'm showing and everything, and he still had the nerve to put his hands on me. He was upset that I still hadn't gotten the abortion, and he was worried that it was too late, but under no circumstances should a man put his hands on a woman, especially while she's carrying his child. He grabbed me by my hair and threw me onto the floor. He told me that if I didn't get rid of my baby on my own, he would do it for me. Well, I snapped. I told him that I was going to have the baby and introduce him to his brothers and see how his wife would react. That did it. He took both of his huge, masculine hands and wrapped them around my neck so tight. I was sure I would die right there in his arms. That's the one time I can say I was thankful he had a wife, because she called his cell phone at that very moment. She told him she needed him to come home because one of their sons had a fever. He left immediately. And somehow, I feel like I owe that woman my life.' "

Monica closed the diary and let it fall in her lap. She held her face in her hands and cried. She was learning things about her husband that scared her. How could a man she knew so well lead another life as someone she didn't know at all? It was a hard pill to swallow. Carlos had been more than a good husband to her, and the love they shared for each other was immeasurable. She could not understand how he could do the things the diary described. She badly wanted to write it all off, but the information and the details the woman provided made that impossible.

Immediately, she started thinking of all the times Carlos had made excuses to be away from her, all the times he came home late from work, and all the times he didn't answer his cell phone. She was sure he was with his mistress on those occasions. She then started thinking about all the good times she and Carlos spent together and how he kept her extremely happy and how great a father he was. Was it all done to keep her blinded from his affair? Was it was all an act? He had been playing one role with her and another with his mistress all to be able to have his cake and eat it too. And I fell right into it, she thought, I should have known he was too good to be true.

Rita had been rubbing Monica on her back as she cried. "It's going to be all right. Once you talk to Carlos and hear what he has to say about this, and you calm down some, I bet he'll clear this up, and we'll all look back at this day and laugh. Just put the book on hold until after you talk to your husband. It could all be a misunderstanding," Rita said, desperate to comfort her friend.

Monica shook her head from left to right and mumbled, "I have to know everything before I approach him."

Straightening up and wiping away her tears with her trembling hands, she retrieved the diary from between her knees and opened it again.

Her voice shaking uncontrollably and light tears escaping her eyes, she read, " 'March 30th, 2003. Dear Diary: I thought I would be over Carlos after not having any dealings with him for so long. After that night in my apartment, back in October, I didn't want shit to do with his crazy ass. And I guess the feeling was mutual because he hasn't called me at all. He didn't even call to see if I had went through with terminating my pregnancy. I'm glad though. He probably would have really killed me after seeing that I never got the abortion. I was almost six months pregnant when I finally consulted a doctor, and he talked me out of it. Thank God. He said I was too far along and it would be too risky. He went over all of my other options, and adoption seemed to be the best thing for the baby and me. So for the remainder of my pregnancy I avoided Carlos. I couldn't let him see me pregnant. I was fearful of what he might do. But I wish I didn't have to go through that experience alone. I had terrible morning, noon, and night sickness in my first trimester. Then in my third trimester, I developed what they call gestational diabetes. I was considered high-risk and had to eat a special diet and give myself finger pricks to check my sugar all the time. Then, on top of all that, I was depressed, wishing I hadn't made the mistake of involving a child in my mess. As bad as I wanted a baby, I regretted getting pregnant under such fucked-up circumstances. I beat myself up about it. I was miserable, and I felt so alone. I didn't have anyone in my corner. And the couple of people who may have been helpful, like my sister and my housekeeper, I avoided out of embarrassment. I didn't want anyone to know that I was pregnant, especially by a married man who wanted nothing to do with my baby. I thought I could get through the nine months and give the baby up without anybody ever knowing. Then I had the nerve to believe I could just get on with my life as if it never happened. I was so wrong. I had Carla Sabrina on March 11th, 2003, at three o'clock in the morning. She was adorable. I never thought I could love another human being as much I loved that baby. For a few seconds after having her I forgot about everything. Looking down at her in my arms, it felt like all my problems had disappeared. I forgot about Carlos and all the bullshit he put me through. I forgot about my recent depression, and I even forgot about agreeing to adoption. Well, maybe I just suppressed all of that. When it came time to give my daughter up, I cried for three days straight. It was the biggest mistake of my life. And to think it was all for a man who could care less about me. Now, I have to live with this—and I have to live with it alone.' "

Chapter 6

Angela was sitting on a park bench with her legs crossed and arms folded, watching her fellow residents who were gathered in a circle, clapping their hands, swaying side to side, and chanting, "Go Peggy, go Peggy, go!" to the beat of Rob Base's "It Takes Two."

She was bored. She couldn't believe that she was spending a beautiful Labor Day institutionalized. She would have much rather been at home trying to hook up with Carlos, even if it took begging or a made-up story about needing a workout tape. She thought about the diary she had Vanessa mail. She wondered if it reached its destination, and if so, whether Monica read it. She wished she had called Carlos to see what state he was in. If he was arguing with Monica, it would have told in his voice, and she would have been able to offer support. Then she would have the chance to prove to Carlos how much she really loved him and was willing to do anything to be with him. He would be able to appreciate that, she thought.

"Come on, Angie," Vanessa said as she danced over to Angela, motioning for her to join the group.

Angela frowned and shook her head no. "I can't dance," she said.

"Yeah, right," Vanessa said, as she grabbed Angela's arm, forcing it to unfold, and pulled her to her feet.

"Go, Angie. It's your birthday, not a holiday, but do it anyway," Vanessa sang as she held Angela's arms up and waved them side to side.

The radio started playing "Push It" by Salt-N-Pepa, and Angela loosened up. "Aw, they playin' all the old-school hits," Angela said, starting to do the bump with Vanessa.

Before long Angela and Vanessa were dancing to every song, doing all types of old-school moves—from the Whop and the Butt to the M.C. Hammer and the Cabbage Patch. Haywood from the kitchen had the grill lit up. Everybody around her was smiling and dancing. Even the young girl with whom she had words earlier cheered her on when it was her turn to go down the Soul Train line. She felt like she was at a family reunion with real family. It was a feeling that she'd missed ever since her parents were killed in a car accident when she was fourteen. She couldn't even recall feeling that good and that complete during her seven-year marriage.

"Hello," Rita answered her phone.

"Hey, Rita, how you doin', it's Carlos. By any chance, have you spoken to Monica today? I dropped her off to unpack and she's gone," Carlos explained.

"She's here," Rita said nonchalantly.

Carlos sighed with relief and asked to speak with his wife. Monica was hesitant about taking the phone. She didn't want Carlos to charm her out of being mad. She decided to take the call, but she intended to make the conversation short.

"Carlos, I'm staying here with Rita for a little while, just until I can cool off." Monica got straight to the point.

"What? What are you talking about? Cool off from what?" Carlos asked, completely confused.

"I know all about the affair, but now is not the time to discuss it. I don't want the boys to know. I don't want my mother to know. I just want to stay here with Rita for a while until I can work things out in my head," Monica calmly explained.

"I don't understand, Monica. What affair?" Carlos asked.

Monica was getting angrier just hearing her husband's voice.

"The got damn affair. The Christmas in Langhorne. The big case you had to work on while I was in Texas. *The pregnancy you wanted terminated!* Do you want me to spell it out for you, Carlos? The fucking affair!" Monica replied, her voice rising in anger.

"You watch way too many talk shows," Carlos said with a smirk in his voice.

That was the wrong thing to say because it set Monica off.

"Yeah, that's what you think, isn't it? Isn't that what you told her! I do nothing but sit on the couch watching talk show after talk show! Well, what about when I'm cleaning your house, or cooking your dinner, or washing your clothes? Or what about when I'm tending to your children, bathing them, clothing them, feeding them, occupying them? All that after an eight-hour day! What the hell do you call that? I've been a good wife to you, Carlos! And a damn good mother to Carlos Jr. and Christopher! And this is what you do to me? Why, Carlos? Why did you feel the need to get another woman? What did she do for you that I didn't? What was worth losing your family?"

There was a long pause.

"ANSWER ME, DAMN IT!" Monica screamed into the phone.

"Monica," Carlos said.

"WHAT?"

"Monica, I don't have a clue what you're talking about. Why don't you just come home so we can figure this out. Apparently someone has been lying to you. And Rita's house is not the place to find out the truth."

"CARLOS, YOU'RE THE ONLY ONE WHO HAS BEEN LYING TO ME! YOU'VE BEEN SLEEPING WITH ANOTHER WOMAN AND COMING HOME TO ME!"

"Monica, I swear to you I haven't been messing around. We just came from a beautiful vacation celebrating—"

"Oh, was that to celebrate? Or was that done out of guilt? Because I must say, I have been a little suspicious of all the extreme niceness lately."

"Suspicious? Monica, I bent my back over for you our entire marriage. This *niceness* that you're talkin' about didn't just arrive. And I worked hard to pull off that surprise vacation for our anniversary! Our tenth anniversary, which is *today*! If I felt guilty about anything, I'm sure I could have just bought you some flowers and wiped my slate clean. I mean, you and I both know it don't take much to make you happy," Carlos said.

"What are you tryin' to say, Carlos?"

"Are you listening? I DON'T KNOW WHAT RITA IS OVER THERE TELLIN' YOU, BUT I DIDN'T CHEAT ON YOU, AND I'M NOT CHEATING ON YOU!" Carlos shouted.

"Don't put Rita in this. She's not the reason for this. If anything, she's on your side." Monica retorted.

"Then where in the hell are you getting this shit from?" Carlos asked, frustrated.

Monica started to cry, "She sent me her diary. Carlos, just tell me why," Monica sobbed, "we were happy, weren't we?"

"Baby, we are happy. This must be a misunderstanding. I don't know what you are talking about. A diary? Baby, I'm just as confused as you. I don't wanna argue like this anymore. Come home," Carlos said.

Monica pulled the phone away from her ear and let it dangle in her hand for a moment. She shook her head from left to right slowly as she wiped her eyes with her spare hand. Meanwhile Rita sat on the couch watching Monica's every move. Monica spoke into the phone once again.

"Okay," Monica whispered softly in between sniffling.

"We'll straighten everything out when you get here," Carlos said, sounding a bit satisfied.

"All right," Monica said.

"I love you, you hear me?" Carlos assured his wife.

"I love you too," Monica sighed.

"Come home," Carlos repeated.

"Okay," Monica said as she hung up.

"You want me to take you home?" Rita asked, sensing Monica wanted to reconcile.

Monica shook her head no and said, "I can't, Rita, not until I know everything."

Rita stood up and walked over to her friend. She hugged her. Monica's body sank into Rita's arms as she wept.

"Everything's going to be fine," Rita said, consoling Monica. "I'm here for you," she added.

Chapter 7

Rita was sitting on the couch eating a turkey sandwich and listening to her sister, Beverly, talk about the fun she was having at her cookout.

"Mom and Dad over here getting tipsy. And Johnny brought one of those blow-up bouncer things for the kids. They lovin' it. I wish you were here. I need some help in this kitchen," Beverly ran down.

"What you cookin'?" Rita asked.

"Honey, I'm fryin' me some salmon—"

"Fryin' salmon?"

"Yeah, girl, with that deep fryer Johnny bought me last Valentine's Day. They taste good too. Almost like mackerel cakes."

"You gotta put me up a plate," Rita said, taking a bite out of her sandwich. The sun had moved from her side of the street to the other, and she was somewhat disappointed in how her day had ended up. She had planned to be at Beverly's for their family's cookout. And she would have loved to be the taste tester of that fried salmon. But since Rita was Monica's only best friend and confidante, she felt obligated to stay in the house consoling her. Besides, if the shoe were on the other foot, she knew Monica would have done the same.

Dear Diary, Monica began to read to herself.

>*I smiled today for the first time in a long time. I was hesitant, but I called Carlos. He still had the same number. He didn't answer. He was with his wife, obviously, because he never answered blocked calls whenever he was with her. But he responded to the brief message I left. He was surprised to hear from me. He thought I had moved on with my life. I told him I'd thought we could use some time apart. We were getting too wrapped in each other, and it was causing us problems. He agreed. We spoke for a short time and made plans for the weekend. He told me to meet him at the airport with enough clothes for three days. I was shocked but enthused. I couldn't wait to see what Carlos had planned. I wondered where he was taking me. But I didn't ask questions. I just rode with the plan.*

>*Dear Diary,*

>*Never in a million years did I expect the surprise Carlos had for me. I met him at the airport on Friday morning at ten A.M. as planned. We grabbed a quick bite for breakfast and got on our eleven fifteen flight. We arrived at Miami International Airport at about one thirty.*

"The son of a bitch," Monica said under her breath as she proceeded to read.

There was a rented stretch Hummer waiting for us. During our drive, he told me that he didn't call me in all these past six months because he was so ashamed of himself for putting his hands on me. He said he was going to try hard to make up for that night. We drove to a café for lunch. Miami was gorgeous and so were all of its residents. I felt like I was in Hollywood—everybody looked like a model, men and women. Carlos and myself fit right in. We made a cute couple, I thought. His Latino background produced some strong features, and his career assured his physical fitness. I think that's one of the reasons we clicked so well. We had a lot in common. He was a personal trainer, and I was very much into working out and staying physically fit. We could benefit from each other and complement each other at the same time. We ate and talked and reminisced about old times. I didn't ask about his wife or their relationship status, even though I wanted to. I didn't want to spoil the mood. We drove some miles to Fort Lauderdale.

"They went to see his mom. And I bet that evil lady was happy to see him with someone else," Monica said angrily.

Carlos's mom was surprised to see us. She wasn't expecting a visit from her son, and she was especially surprised to see him with me. I was surprised, myself. Carlos didn't tell me that we were visiting his mother. I guess he knew that I would have had a problem with that. I mean, I was the man's mistress. It wasn't my place to meet his mom. I was flattered, though. And she was pretty nice to me, so I didn't feel too uncomfortable. We stayed with her for a little while, enough time for Carlos to prepare dinner. I had no idea Carlos could cook like that. He was a gourmet chef. He made some grilled chicken, cinnamon mashed carrots, and dirty rice. I was enjoying myself. But the best was yet to come. After dinner and dessert Carlos and I got in the Hummer and were driven the two hours to Marco Island, where Carlos had rented a house. It was a three-story villa positioned right on the beach. I was in awe. Carlos was winning my heart all over again. For a minute I felt like Mrs. Carlos Vasquez. Monica who?

"OH MY GOD, RITA," Monica shouted. "He took the bitch to Marco Island where he just took me for our anniversary!"

Rita looked over at Monica and quickly brought her conversation with her sister to an end. "Bev, let me call you back. Tell the kids auntie'll be over, and tell Mom and Dad hey. All right. 'Bye." Rita hung up the phone. "No the fuck he didn't," Rita said to Monica right after pressing the off button on her cordless phone.

"Yes, he did. He had the stretch Hummer and everything. I just read it. After they left his mom's."

"I don't know, Monica. This doesn't sound like Carlos. To take another woman around his mom."

"Well, how would she know about this? How would she know where his mother lives? And the Marco Island trip? We just got back. How would she know about that unless he took her. This motherfucker done lost his mind. Taking her to see his mom and shit," Monica snapped.

"All right, enough is enough. I haven't heard you cuss this much since junior high. Close that damn book. You know all you need to know. Now, she's got you right where she wants you, all mad and heartbroken. Don't you know, misery loves company. She wants your husband, and you are about to grant her that wish by falling out over this damn diary," Rita explained.

"I could care less! I don't even want Carlos after all of this. At this point I just wanna know everything. The more shit he did, the more shit I can get his ass for in divorce court," Monica said, finding the place where she left off in the diary.

"Well, you got a point there," Rita said before disappearing into her kitchen. Monica read silently.

The next morning Carlos woke me up to breakfast in bed. The sun had risen and the seagulls were squawking. The sound of the waves crashing against the shore was so soothing. I ate the cheese omelet and side of sausage and drank the cappuccino. I had it all. A good-looking man and a good cook. All that was missing was the good sex but that wasn't for long. That evening I fulfilled a fantasy of mine. Carlos and I made love on the beach. There's nothing in the world more passionate.

"Rita, take me home please!" Monica shouted as she shut the diary.

Rita reentered the living room. She looked at Monica, not knowing what to say or do. Go home, stay away. Monica was so volatile, Rita didn't know whether she was coming or going.

"They had sex on the beach," Monica whined. "Can you imagine, Rita? You're home taking care of a man's children while he's sticking his dick in some stranger."

"Um, Monica, I don't know what to tell you, honey," Rita said, not knowing how to help her friend.

"There's nothing you can tell me, Rita, I'm going to go home and beat the shit out of Carlos," Monica said, beginning to cry again. "How could he go so low?" she asked, wailing.

Ring! Ring!

Rita looked at her cordless phone before answering.

"It's Carlos," she said calmly.

"Tell him I'm not coming home. Tell him don't even think about me coming home 'cause it's not going to happen," Monica demanded.

"Hello," Rita answered.

"Rita, it's Carlos. Has Monica left yet?"

"Carlos, Monica said she isn't ready to go home. Just give her some time, okay?" Rita said, sounding tired.

Frustrated, Carlos asked, "What is going on, Rita? What are you over there telling her?"

"I'm not telling her anything. She's reading it all in that stupid diary."

"What's this diary she's talking about?" Carlos asked, his voice desperate.

"The diary she told you about earlier. The diary of your mistress," Rita said with an attitude.

There was a long silence. Carlos was putting two and two together. The first thought that came to his head was Angela.

"Rita," Carlos said with urgency, "you have to get that diary from her. You can't let her keep reading it! It's all lies!"

"Carlos, I've been trying to tell her that since she first told me about it. I don't think it's a good idea for her to keep reading the damn thing either. But she read some stuff that sounds pretty official. And she's not going to put it down until she's read the last page," Rita explained.

"I'm telling you, Rita, it's all bullshit. Tell my wife to come home and I'll explain it all to her—the truth," Carlos pleaded.

"What is he still on the phone for? Tell him I'll be home when I'm ready to be home!" Monica shouted loud enough for Carlos to hear her in the background.

"You heard her?" Rita asked Carlos.

"Hang up the phone, Rita!" Monica shouted again.

"You heard her. I have to go," Rita said to Carlos, and hung up in his ear.

Monica turned to Rita and asked, "What the hell does he care if I read the rest of the diary for? It can't get any worse."

"What good is it doing you, though? Some things are better left unknown, don't you think?" Rita asked, trying again to get Monica to stop reading.

"Rita, if you had a husband and a woman sent you something like this, you would read the whole thing too, maybe even twice. Yeah, it hurts like hell to find out so much and in such detail, but as a woman, as a wife, you would just want to know everything, especially if you never suspected anything," Monica explained.

Rita accepted Monica's explanation and gave up trying to get her to close the diary. "Well, can I get you something? Some water?" Rita asked.

"Yes, a glass of water, please," Monica said as she reopened the diary.

Dear Diary,

I didn't think I would be visiting Florida again so soon. But when Carlos asked me for moral support, I had to attend his mother's funeral. I must admit, I was jealous. Carlos sat up front with his wife and their sons. They looked like a happy family, and the way Carlos was with his sons made me wish he had chosen to be that way with our child. Hell, he didn't even know we had a child. He thought I aborted the baby. I sat in the back of the funeral home and paid my respects quietly. I didn't go up to view the body. I was just there for Carlos. I couldn't understand his logic for wanting me there while his wife was there, but I was so deeply in love with him that it didn't even matter. If he wanted me somewhere, I was going to be there. I just wondered if he felt the same way. Anyway, after the funeral, Carlos and his family went to their hotel. Carlos had set it up for me to have a room a few floors up from them. Although I was the third leg, I found it quite exciting. He came up to my room in the middle of the night. He had told his wife that he went out for drinks with his brother. I wondered if he felt any guilt. I was beginning to peel away the bullshit with Carlos. When we first got together, he convinced me that he was so unhappy with her that he was seeking a divorce. But that was damn near four years ago, and his ass still hasn't signed no papers. Plus, I can tell that he's happy with his wife just by the way he looked at her at the funeral. It's like they just met when he looks at her. So I tried not to think of a future with Carlos like I did in the past. I tried to convince myself that our relationship was much better and much more fun with no strings attached. I tried to hold back my feelings and just look at my affair with Carlos as a roller-coaster ride. It would be thrilling. It would be a bit bumpy. It would be fun. And it would be brief.

Rita placed a glass of water on the end table beside Monica.

"Rita, do you remember any women at Carlos's mother's funeral who were alone?" Monica quizzed as she sipped the water.

Rita frowned as she thought back to the funeral.

"I hardly remember anybody at that funeral. That was over a year ago, why?"

"She was there," Monica said calmly as she continued reading.

The sun was going down. The staff members at Taylor's had their hands full with condiments and leftover food as they led the residents inside the building.

"I had so much fun," Angela told Vanessa as they walked side by side through the automatic doors.

"It was fun, wasn't it," Vanessa agreed. "I ain't partied that hard since my college days."

"You and me both. I needed that. I feel like a whole new woman," Angela said.

"That's good. Hopefully the judge will let you go home tomorrow."

"Wouldn't that be the icing on the cake," Angela said.

Vanessa nodded her head and exhaled as the elevator approached their floor. The group of about seven poured off the elevator and followed the shift leader through the door of their unit. Vanessa went straight to her station and gathered her belongings.

"Well, good night everybody. I had a good time today. I'll see y'all tomorrow," Vanessa said.

Angela stopped Vanessa with a hug.

"Just in case I'm not here when you come in tomorrow, thank you so much for everything. You really made this past week easy on me. I don't know how I would have kept it together without you."

Vanessa smiled and told Angela to take care of herself. She wished her luck and continued out the door.

Angela walked down the hall and into her room. She sat down on her bed and stared at the stark white wall. Her thoughts instantly went to Carlos. I wonder what Carlos is doing right now. Is Monica going upside his head yet? Did she leave the house and go to her mom's? If so, I hope she took the boys. I don't want Carlos to have any excuses when I tell him I want to see him tomorrow. I hope he doesn't get mad at me right away. He shouldn't. He should understand that I did what I did to be with him. And he should appreciate the fact that I made it easier for him to get a divorce. He'll probably be crying when I call him. I hope so. I will tell him to meet me at my house so we can talk about it. When he gets there, I'll have candles lit, dinner ready, and be in my sexiest outfit. He'll forget all about Monica, and when she serves him those papers, he'll sign without hesitating. Oh God, I can't wait.

Angela knelt down on the floor and put her elbows on her bed. She bowed her head and prayed: Thank you, God, for all of your true and wonderful blessings. Thank you for a good day. Thank you for getting me through this week. Dear God, please let everything go my way tomorrow. Please let my sister and Dr. Whitaker be there. Please let the panel recognize that I have changed. Please let them see my improvement, and please let them discharge me. Please let Carlos take my calls. I need to see him. I need to hear his voice. I need to be near him. God, you know, I've never loved a man like I love Carlos. Please, God, make him see that and make him love me back. Amen.

Chapter 8

Rita pressed the guide button on her TV remote. The time in the left-hand corner said nine thirty-five. Monica had been at Rita's house all day long, reading, eating, crying, arguing with Carlos, and occasionally venting to Rita, who had grown exhausted.

"I'm going to put on my pajamas. You want me to bring you down something to put on?" Rita asked as she stood up from the couch and stretched.

"No, I'm okay," Monica mumbled without looking up from the diary.

"You want a blanket, a pillow, anything?" Rita asked.

"No, I'll be fine," Monica said, turning another page.

Dear Diary,

Just when things were going well, I had to fuck it up. I gave Carlos crabs and when I finally told him, he had already given them to his wife and his kids. I felt so ashamed, so embarrassed, and so bad for his kids. That damn David. I knew I should have stopped dealing with him. I knew it was his nasty ass who had given it to me. Carlos didn't know what he was going to tell his wife when she got home from the doctor. She had her and the kids checked out, and when the doctor told her it was crabs, she flipped. She called Carlos while he was at work, cursing him out. He didn't even get a chance to get a word out. I told him that that was good because it gave him time to find a good excuse without having to come up with something off the top of his head. I did some research and told Carlos to tell his wife that he had got it from a toilet seat at the gym where he works. That was logical. Shit, so many different people come in and out of gyms, it's not uncommon to catch something from somebody. And it wasn't like he had syphilis or something that you can only get from sex. Crabs can come from different things, not necessarily sex. She believed him, but only after she did some research on her own and double-checked with her doctor. I thought Carlos was going to tell me he didn't want to deal with me anymore after that. But he took it better than I thought he would. I guess because it didn't put a dent in his re-lationship with his wife. But his kids, though. I know how much he loves those boys, and I would think he would be ready to fuck me up for putting them in that position. But all he did was make me promise that from then on I would have sex only with him. How ironic, his married, cheatin' ass ask-ing me, a single woman, for monogamy.

Monica closed the book and gripped it in her hands. She squeezed the book with all her might until her hands hurt.

"Rita!" Monica shouted.

Rita rushed back down the steps. "What, Monica?" Rita asked, worry all over her face.

Monica just sat silently and still while tears poured down her cheeks. She thought back to the time her doctor had told her that she had crabs. She thought back to the looks on her sons' faces as she put the shampoo on their little bodies. She felt so bad, like she had failed as a mother. She wished she could have protected her children from shit like that. But she never expected to have to protect them from their own father.

"Monica, what? What did he do?" Rita asked, still waiting for a response, trying to break Monica out of the zone she was in.

"He gave my children crabs, Rita," Monica said slowly and dazedly, as if she were in a trance.

"What do you mean?" Rita asked, her face scrunched up.

Monica began to explain, "He told me he got them from the gym. The doctor even told me that it was possible. But he really got them from her and brought them home to me and my kids."

Rita's face produced a look of sorrow as she shook her head in disbelief. She didn't have any children, but C.J. and Chris were her godsons, and she loved them like they were hers. She didn't know what to say to Monica. What do you say to something like that, Rita thought, as she shuffled through her mind trying to find the right words.

"I never told you or anybody because I was embarrassed. Plus, I didn't want to hear the negative thoughts. You know, people telling me that it was bullshit that he got crabs from the gym," Monica said, still staring into space.

"Well, how did he give them to Chris and C.J.?" Rita was confused and curious.

"That's the thing about crabs; they can get in bed-sheets and clothes. That's why I believed his ass when he told me he got them from the gym. Even the doctor said he could have gotten them from a toilet seat or some equipment," Monica told Rita.

Monica wiped her face with her hands. She looked over at Rita, shaking her head. "Rita," she sang, as if she was warning Rita of something, "he really did it with this one."

Monica's left leg was shaking vigorously. She was furious. She loved her two kids to death and would kill for them, as she thought any mother would. She kept picturing the time when her sons would scratch and squirm, irritated by their condition. She wasn't concerned so much about herself, it was her children she felt bad for. How could he bring something my kids' way and then continue on with that bitch like it was nothing? How trifling is that, Monica thought.

Rita was shocked speechless. If Monica had kept the crabs situation from her, Rita was sure there were other incidents that may have pointed to Carlos's cheating that Monica had failed to tell her about as well.

"And this is the man I trusted with my life. The way shit is being spread these days, I could have gotten AIDS from him, my own husband. It's not supposed to be like that. A married woman—or man, for that matter—should not have to worry about shit like that. I shouldn't have to make my own husband wear a condom. That's a part of what marriage is all about; it's sacred. You should be able to trust your spouse with your life," Monica vented. "I need to talk to my kids," Monica said, reaching for the phone. "I need to hear their voices."

Monica dialed the number to her house, and C.J. picked up.

"Hello," C.J. said softly.

"Hi, honey," Monica sang, sniffling like she had a cold.

"Mom-my," C.J. sang back. "Where are you? You coming home?" he asked.

"Mommy is visiting Pop-Pop," Monica lied. "I'll be home in the morning bright and early with breakfast for you and your brother."

"Chocolate-chip pancakes?" C.J. asked excitedly.

"Whatever you want," Monica said. "Now let me speak to Christopher."

"Hold on," C.J. said.

"Hello." Monica heard Christopher's voice.

"Hey, Chris," Monica said, trying hard to keep from crying. "You and C.J. get ready for bed, and Mommy will see you in the morning when she leaves Pop-Pop's. I love you two, and I want you both to have sweet dreams, okay?"

"Okay, Mommy, we love you too," Christopher said.

"Monica, don't hang up," Carlos butted in. "Hello?"

Monica heard Carlos's voice, but she hung up anyway. Rita took the phone from her and put it on the receiver. She then began locking her house, closing windows and curtains, and getting ready for bed. Meanwhile, Monica sat in the same spot, seemingly paralyzed, her eyes glued to the pages of Angela's diary.

Dear Diary,

I want to scream! Matter of fact, I am screaming! All right, let me slow down and catch my breath. I want to start from the beginning. Carlos invited me to dinner. We went to the Cheesecake Factory. Nothing too fabulous, but nice enough. Right after we had our entrées, while we were waiting for our dessert, our waiter told me I had a phone call. I was confused, not knowing who could possibly be calling me. My sister didn't know I was there, and there was no one else in my life who would bother to call me at home let alone at a restaurant. I excused myself from the table and followed the waiter to the phone.

As soon as I picked up and said hello, a voice on the other end recited the words, "Will you marry me?" All I could do was smile. I couldn't even answer, I was so happy. I was frozen in place. The waiter then came over to me with a small crystal jar of mints. He held it out to me and asked if I would like one. I looked in the jar, still holding the phone to my ear. There was a gorgeous diamond engagement ring. I held my hand over my mouth. My eyes lit up like stars. The waiter took the ring out of the jar and placed it on my finger. Meanwhile, Carlos was on the other end of the phone waiting for my response. Well? he asked me. I told him yes. Then we met in the middle of the restau-

rant, where we hugged each other tight. Waiters and waitresses were clapping, and people were congratulating us. Little did everybody know, Carlos already had a wife.

"He proposed to his mistress, bought her a diamond ring and all. And did it at the Cheesecake Factory at that," Monica said, apparently unfazed.

"What if somebody you knew was in there and seen his trifling ass proposing to some other chick?" Rita asked, disgusted.

"I guess it didn't matter to him. He must have thought he was invincible by this time. He had done so much before this and got away with it," Monica hypothesized.

"Monica, you need to divorce his ass so fast," Rita said, completely pissed off.

"Oh, trust me, it's done. First thing in the morning," Monica affirmed.

"Take his ass for everything you can," Rita said. "And I thought there was at least one good man left in this world," she added.

"Believe me, Rita, I thought so too. Carlos never really gave me any reasons to think he was having an affair. He was like the perfect husband. How could he do this? I mean, he had to feel guilty at some point, right?" Monica asked, trying to make sense of her husband's behavior.

"Well, shit, he probably didn't feel guilty because you were so happy. As long as you and those kids had a smile on y'alls faces, and were well taken care of, he was satisfied. What he did on the side didn't affect his household, so he probably felt like it was just fine," Rita said, drawing her own conclusion.

"But proposing to the woman? That's going a little too far, don't you think?" Monica asked.

"Well, did he really plan on marrying her? And if so, why didn't he? Shit, what you really need to know is when the affair ended and why." Rita pointed out.

"I don't even know that it did end," Monica retorted.

"Oh, trust me, it ended. Otherwise she wouldn't have sent you this shit. He must have really pissed her off for her to pull a stunt like this," Rita stated with confidence.

Monica reopened the diary to the page where she had left off. Rita had a point. Monica wanted to know when her husband had broken the relationship off and why. She read on.

Chapter 9

It was almost midnight. Rita was stretched out on her sofa, sound asleep. The house was completely dark with the exception of the blue tint that kept switching from bright to dark on the TV and a dim light from a side-table lamp next to Monica's chair. She was still scrunched up in the same recliner she had been in for hours. And she was still reading.

Dear Diary,

The shit is hitting the fan. Carlos has really fucked up now. I don't understand him. One minute we're perfect and he's doing everything right. Then the next minute he does something that threatens our relationship. We were planning our wedding. I know, I know, his ass should have been planning a divorce. But that was to be taken care of well before our date. Anyway, we were happy with each other. It was like we went back to the beginning before any drama. We were going out a lot, eating, seeing movies, going to comedy shows and concerts. We were spending a lot of time together. His wife thought he was in San Diego on business for two months. He had told her he was offered a deal from a production company on the West Coast to shoot his own workout video. She was so happy for him. She knew that it was always his dream to have his own workout videos. It was big money in that. Anyway, he wasn't in California for those two months. He was living with me. We wanted to try it out and see how we would get along cohabitating, especially before the wedding. It went fine too. But no sooner did he leave my house than he did something to fuck up everything. I got a phone call from him one night. He said he needed to see me really bad, and he had something he wanted to talk to me about. I got out of my bed—mind you, it was three o'clock in the morning—and I met him at Silk City. We sat down and placed our orders. I knew Carlos had done something stupid just from the look on his face. He looked so sad, almost depressed. I kept asking him what was the problem, but he procrastinated answering me. So after a while I said to hell with it. He'll tell me when he's ready. We ate our food and drank our hot chocolates. Then we sat in silence, both stuffed as pigs. I would glance at him every few seconds to see if he was ready to talk. But he said nothing. He just glanced back at me, occasionally reaching across the table to caress my hands. He finally decided to open his mouth after stroking his goatee a few times. He started off by telling me the obvious. He had fucked up. I told him I figured that much. He proceeded to tell me just how he had fucked up, and this was the part that I wasn't prepared for. He told me that he slept with someone else. Now I know it was not my place to be upset, considering I was well aware of the fact that I wasn't his one and only. But somehow, I felt some type of way. I felt like I had been cheated on. In a way I had, though. I mean, I was wearing a ring and planning a wedding with this man. Anyway, I swallowed my pride and just listened. I didn't snap on him like I wanted to. Shit, if he wanted somebody to flip out on him he would have gone home and told his wife, so I pretended it was all right. He was confiding in me as a friend, so I had to play my part as such. I had to step outside of the fiancée role. But when he told me that he had just finished and that was where he was coming from, the "bitch" came flying out of me. I gave him a look that could have killed his ass. I walked out of the diner without saying a word to him. I couldn't stand to look at him knowing he had just got finished fucking somebody else and it wasn't his wife. He followed me to my car, begging for my forgiveness. I wanted to know one thing. Who was she? He told me to think back to his mother's funeral. He told me it was the woman who sat beside his wife. He told me that was why he felt so bad and that was why he couldn't go home. He could fuck me all he wanted and still face his wife with a smile. But he had just fucked her best friend. Now that was a different story. He didn't know how he would be able to face his wife after that.

Monica stopped reading and looked up over at her sleeping friend. Her mouth dropped as she tried to piece together what she had just read. Maybe I read it wrong, she thought. Maybe she's talking about some other woman. There were plenty of women at his mom's funeral. She continued reading.

> *I asked him why he did it. What made him sleep with his wife's best friend. He couldn't give me a reason. He said he was a little tipsy. But he and I both knew that wasn't an excuse. I was confused myself. I could see if this broad looked better than his wife or something. But she didn't have anything on Monica. She was short and round, with no pizzazz. I met her one day when she came to the gym. He told her I was one of his clients. She was cute in the face but overweight, and his wife looked a lot better. That made me realize that men didn't cheat for better but for different.*

Monica was in complete disarray. She didn't want to believe that her best friend had slept with her husband. She kept trying to convince herself that it was another woman, not Rita, who was being talked about in the diary. But Rita was short and round, and she was the only woman sitting next to Monica at Carlos's mother's funeral. And she was Monica's only best friend. She had associates, of course, but only one best friend. So who else could this woman be describing? No one. It was simple. Rita had slept with Carlos. Monica let the information register. She kept repeating it over and over again in her head until she felt herself getting sick.

Monica looked up again at Rita sleeping. She was so comfortable and peaceful, probably dreaming sweet, Monica thought. How could she get any sleep knowing what she had done? Who the hell did she think she was, criticizing Carlos and being ready to fight this woman for messing with my husband, when she had done the very same thing? How dare she talk down about Carlos or his mistress? She was my best fucking friend. My husband was going to be a damn dog regardless, but *she* was my best friend. There's no excusing her, Monica thought.

"Rita," Monica said, as she crossed the room and tapped her friend's shoulder.

Rita opened her eyes slowly. She managed to lift her head just a little as she woke up from a cozy sleep. "Hahn?" she whispered.

Whop! Monica punched Rita right in her face, knocking her head back down on the pillow it had previously been resting on. For a minute Rita was dazed. She thought she was dreaming. She finally got herself together and managed to get on her feet. Feeling moisture on her upper lip, she gently touched her nose then looked at her finger. She was bleeding. In total shock, she looked over at Monica, who was standing a short distance away with her fists balled and legs planted in a fighting stance.

"What the fuck was that about?" Rita asked, bewildered.

Monica was mad. As a matter of fact, she was beyond mad. She picked up the lamp that had provided the dim light by which she had read the diary.

"What are you doing? MONICA, HAVE YOU LOST YOUR FUCKIN' MIND?" Rita screamed.

Monica threw the lamp at her friend, just missing her. "MONICA!" Rita shouted.

Rita positioned herself as if she was ready to fight. She didn't know what was going on, and she really didn't want to have to hurt her girlfriend, but she had to defend herself.

"Come on, bitch!" Monica said, tears beginning to fall down her face.

Rita was confused. "What the fuck is up with you? What are you trippin' over?" Rita asked, trying to avoid any further physical contact.

"You fucked Carlos, didn't you!" Monica shouted.

Rita had a stunned look on her face. She never expected that.

"Didn't you, you fuckin' ho. You fuckin' trick," Monica wept.

Rita didn't know what to say. Her mind was racing. She was worried about her friend, but she was worried about her house and herself as well. She didn't want it to come down to her and Monica rolling around like some simple-ass little girls in the middle of her living room. But she wasn't about to let Monica fuck up her house either.

"Monica, calm down and tell me what's going on, okay?" Rita said with frustration.

"No! Fuck that! You fucked my husband! And you call yourself a friend? You ain't no friend of mine! You're a fuckin' whore!" Monica screamed, still weeping.

Rita kept her distance, and despite her anger at the situation, she tried to calm her friend.

"Monica, I am your friend," Rita said, taking a step toward her. "I wouldn't do no shit like that. I knew you since the fourth grade!"

"That's the sad part, Rita! You were my best friend since I was nine years old. You was there when I met Carlos. You was my bridesmaid! You're my kids' god-mom! Don't fuckin' come near me, Rita! I swear to God, Rita. I will fuckin' hurt you!"

Rita took another step toward Monica. She knew Monica was upset, but she doubted her friend would do as she threatened. First of all, Rita was sure she could beat Monica. Monica wasn't the fighting type, and be-sides, Rita had about fifty pounds on her. Second, she didn't believe Monica had it in her to swing on her again.

"Monica," Rita said as she held her arms out as if to hug her.

Monica swung her hands at Rita, and grazed Rita's extended arms.

"GET THE FUCK AWAY FROM ME!" Monica screamed. She picked up a framed picture of Rita that sat on the same side table as the lamp Monica had thrown.

"ALL RIGHT, ENOUGH IS FUCKIN' ENOUGH," Rita shouted, no longer able to control her anger.

"What the fuck are you going to do?" Monica asked, further provoking Rita.

Rita leaped at her friend and grabbed for the picture. But Monica quickly threw the picture at Rita, hitting her in the face. Rita went off. She started swinging on Mon-ica. Monica swung back wildly and out of control. The two of them ended up tumbling over Rita's recliner chair, knocking it on its side, and landing on the floor. Rita was on top, pushing Monica's face into the carpet. Rita had tried to get up off of her, but Monica had a grip on her hair. So, with one hand she held Monica's face to the floor, and with the other she tried to detangle Monica's delicate, manicured fingers from her hair. Rita stood up and quickly reached for the phone. Meanwhile, Monica was getting up and gathering her things that were scattered about, including the diary.

"I'm calling the police," Rita said, out of breath, pressing 911 quickly.

"What the fuck, you gonna have me arrested?" Monica shouted, as she looked around for her pocketbook.

"That's right! I'ma have ya ass arrested," Rita said. She had lost any sympathy she had for Monica. She looked around at her trashed living room and Monica became her worst enemy.

Monica put down the diary and jumped at Rita, starting the fight again. Rita defended herself, raising the phone against Monica's face. Monica tried to block it, but failed. The phone clocked her right in the mouth, drawing blood. Monica was furious. She started swinging on Rita again, striking her all over. The police dispatcher could be heard screaming hello repeatedly, while the phone lay faceup on the floor. All the while Monica and Rita were brawling in the middle of Rita's living room.

Within a short period of time the police arrived at Rita's front door. Rita was right there to greet them.

"GET HER OUT OF HERE! GET HER OUT OF MY HOUSE!" Rita demanded of the police officer.

"Ma'am, would you like to press charges?" one of the officers asked Rita as the other officer removed Monica from Rita's front steps.

Rita thought about it. She knew if she said yes, Monica would be hauled off to jail, and even though she was pissed enough she couldn't care less if Monica spent the night in a cell, she really didn't want that. She still had love for Monica. She was her best friend; she was family.

"No, I don't need to press charges. Just get her the hell away from here," Rita responded.

"Let me get my stuff!" Monica yelled from the pavement.

"Does she have belongings here?" the officer asked Rita.

"Here," Rita said, handing the cop Monica's pocketbook.

"What about my book?" Monica screamed, crying uncontrollably.

Rita walked back inside her house to retrieve the diary.

"Here! Take this shit. It got you going crazy, looking like a damn fool!" Rita shouted. She threw the diary down to Monica from her porch.

The officer put his finger up to his lips, signaling Rita to keep quiet. The other officer picked the diary up off the ground and handed it to Monica.

One officer turned to Monica and began to explain, "Now, she's not gonna press charges. So you won't be going to jail tonight. But you're gonna have to leave her property."

"That's fine. That's fine. I wanna go home. I wanna see my children. I just want my children," Monica cried.

Chapter 10

"What do I owe you?" Monica asked.

The taxi driver pointed to the meter and said, "Five twenty."

Monica pulled her wallet from her pocketbook and counted out seven one-dollar bills. "Here you go," she said, then got out of the cab.

"Thank you," the driver said, before pulling off down the empty street.

Monica walked up her driveway, glancing inside her car as she passed by it. She approached the steps to her house and grew anxious. Through the window she could see that the living room TV was on. She had hoped Carlos would be asleep. She was too upset to face him. She knew that one word out of his mouth was likely to set her off, and she didn't want another fight. But she desperately wanted to see her boys. She needed them in her arms.

Monica carefully unlocked the door, leaving it cracked. She peeked in the living room and noticed Carlos was asleep on the couch. She crept past him and up the stairs into one son's room. "Chris," Monica whispered as she nudged his arm. "Wake up, honey," she said, and she picked Chris up and put him over her shoulder.

"Mommy?" Chris asked, wiping his eyes, still half asleep.

"Yes, baby, it's me," Monica said, holding him tight.

With Chris in her arms, Monica walked down the hall to C.J.'s room. She woke him from his sleep and held his hand, guiding him down the stairs.

"Mom, where are we going?" C.J. asked with a yawn.

"Shh," Monica said. "We don't want to wake up Daddy."

"Monica?" Carlos whispered, as he awakened to see his wife picking up the car keys from the coffee table.

"Monica, what are you doing?" he asked, confused.

Monica ignored her husband. "Chris and C.J, go wait in the car," she said, and she walked over to the front door. She pressed the unlock button on the car's key remote. Carlos followed his wife and sons to the door.

"Monica, what are you doing? It's one o'clock in the morning. The boys need to be in bed."

"Me and the boys are going to my mom's," she told him sternly. Then she mumbled, "Don't act like you know what's best for them. You're the reason they had crabs at three years old!"

Carlos had a confused look on his face.

"Listen, Monica, you need to talk to me and get whatever information straightened out. Our kids don't need to be woken out of their sleep in the middle of the night for this nonsense!" Carlos stated.

Monica knew she was too upset to have a civilized talk with him. She just wanted to take her kids and leave.

"Good-bye, Carlos," Monica said as she started toward the car.

Carlos grabbed Monica's arm and turned her to face him.

"You're not taking my children anywhere this late!"

Monica shrugged away from him. "Don't put your hands on me!"

"What the hell is wrong with you?" Carlos asked, still confused.

"All right!" Monica said. "You wanna know? I can handle you messin' around on me. I can handle you gettin' another woman pregnant. And somehow, I was able to handle the fact that my kids got crabs from their trifling, cheatin'-ass father. But you went and fucked Rita! My best friend for years!"

Carlos was perplexed. "I did none of the above, Monica. Rita? Come on now, I would never disrespect you like that. Somebody lied to you. And until you're ready to hear me out, you are not leaving this house," Carlos said.

"You would say that, Carlos!" Monica said, becoming more upset. "Of course you're gonna deny it! That's what you men do! Now, I don't want to discuss this with you right now. I just need to be with my kids and away from you!" she shouted, and turned away from him.

Carlos grabbed Monica and again she shrugged away from him, this time with more force than before.

"I *SAID* DON'T PUT YOUR HANDS ON ME!" Monica screamed, with hate in her tone.

"Quiet down! We have neighbors, and it's too damn early in the morning!" Carlos said, becoming frustrated as he headed toward the car where Chris and C.J. were sitting in the backseat. "I'm putting the boys back to bed. If you want to take them to your mom's, you can do it tomorrow. They need to be in their beds asleep, not put in the middle of your madness!" Carlos said. He stormed past Monica.

"Leave my kids right where they are!" Monica shouted, and she gripped Carlos's arm.

"They're my kids too!" Carlos said as he broke loose from Monica's grip.

Monica walked up on Carlos and grabbed him by his T-shirt.

"Leave my kids where they are!"

Carlos turned around and shoved Monica slightly. Then he moved to get his children out of the car. But right before he could open the car door, he heard the click of the car's lock mechanism. Monica had pressed the lock button with the remote.

Chris and C.J. looked confused and scared at the sight of their mom and dad fighting.

"Monica, open the got damn doors!" Carlos commanded.

"No! Let us go! I'm not staying here with you tonight! Why can't you accept that?" Monica responded.

"Well, then, you go to your mom's. Leave the kids here!" Carlos ordered.

"I'm not leaving my kids here with you!" Monica shot back, her voice dripping with attitude.

Carlos was beginning to lose his temper, and his patience was wearing thin. He turned around to face his wife, who was a few steps behind him. She tried to brush past him and get in the car, but he wasn't about to let her take his kids. He gripped her and pinned her against the wall, leaving her feet dangling slightly off the ground. He forcefully snatched the car keys out of her hand and then let her go. He pressed the button to open the car doors.

"Y'all go back to bed," Carlos instructed his sons as he approached the car again. "Everything will be all right; your mom and me need to talk."

Meanwhile, Monica yelled, "No! Get back in the car."

Not knowing who to listen to, the twins started to cry.

"This has gone too far!" Carlos shouted, pulling Chris and C.J. from the backseat.

"Mommy," Chris cried out as Carlos breezed past Monica carrying both the boys. Monica followed behind Carlos cursing and screaming: "I CAN'T STAY IN THIS HOUSE WITH YOU! GIVE ME MY KIDS AND THE KEYS AND LET ME LEAVE!" she yelled at the top of her lungs.

All the while, the twins were still crying. Carlos put them down and used his hands to wipe their tears. "Go back to bed," he told them as he walked them up the stairs. Monica continued to fuss, begging Carlos to let her take the keys.

Carlos walked into the kitchen, trying to get away from his wife. He opened the refrigerator, took out a jug of water, and started to drink straight from it. He needed to cool off. Monica entered the kitchen, still at it.

"GIVE ME THE FUCKIN' KEYS! GIVE ME THE FUCKIN' KEYS! LET ME LEAVE! WHY ARE YOU TRYIN' TO KEEP ME HERE! LET ME GO!"

Carlos was sick of hearing Monica rant and rave like she was crazy. With the force of a pitcher throwing a fast-ball, he threw the car keys straight at her. Carlos didn't budge when the keys hit Monica in the face. Instead, he continued drinking from the water jug. Monica was furious already, and getting hit in the face with the keys just added fuel to the fire. She lost control of herself. She lunged at Carlos, knocking him to the floor, and started pounding him in the chest with her fists. He was squirming, struggling to move from beneath her, but it seemed she had the strength of a man. She kept pounding him with her fists, pouring all of her anger out. Eventually Carlos just stopped. His body had shut down. He was unconscious. He was lifeless. Finally, Monica regained control of herself, bringing her hands to a halt. She started experiencing a piercing pain in her hand. Her eyes widened with fear when she realized she was covered in blood. She looked down at Carlos's limp body. It too was bloody, and there were a bunch of puncture wounds in his chest, shoulder, and arm. His eyes were half closed, and his head was drooped sideways.

"Daddy!" Chris and C.J. yelled out from the entrance-way to the kitchen.

Monica quickly stood up and turned to face her sons. She ran over to them and hugged them tight, trying to keep them from seeing what she had done. She backed them out of the kitchen and took them up to the bathroom. Then she ran bathwater as she undressed them individually.

"Oh goodness, Mommy got blood on your clothes," she said softly, tears streaming down her face.

"What happened to Daddy?" the boys asked, frightened.

Monica ignored them, mumbling under her breath. "Mommy's going to get you two nice and clean and in some fresh pajamas."

"Mommy," C.J. whined, "why were you and Daddy fighting?"

"What happened to Daddy?" Chris asked again.

Monica continued to ignore her sons' questions, rambling on about getting them changed. They cried and whined to their mother, asking about their father.

"Is Daddy hurt?" Chris asked.

Monica stopped what she was doing and looked up at Chris. She saw fear in his eyes. She suddenly rushed out of the bathroom, leaving her boys behind.

"Carlos!" Monica yelled over the banister.

"CARLOS! CARLOS!" Monica screamed louder.

Monica began to panic. She rushed into her bedroom and scrambled around in complete darkness, knocking things over and tripping over unpacked luggage looking for the telephone. Meanwhile, the boys' cries could be heard from the bathroom, along with the running water.

Her mind was racing. She needed help. More important, her husband needed help.

"CARLOS! CARLOS!" Monica yelled, hoping for a response.

No response. Monica gave up trying to locate her phone and walked frantically into the bathroom, where she turned off the running water. She grabbed both of her kids and cuddled them into her chest, trying to comfort them.

"Stop crying, everything is all right. Mommy and Daddy are fine. Shh, shh," Monica said, rocking her children in her arms.

"CARLOS!" Monica screamed while still holding her children. "ANSWER ME! CARLOS!"

Monica released her children. "Listen, you two stay in here until I come back upstairs, okay?" She rushed down the steps and went into the kitchen. It was a mess. There was blood everywhere. Glass from the jug was scattered about. Monica made her way carefully through the mess and picked up the kitchen phone. Beside the phone was a note with a phone number written on it, reminding Monica of the dinner reservations she had made for their ten-year wedding anniversary. Her emotional pain worsened.

"Hello," Monica sobbed.

"Hello?"

"Mom!"

"Monica?"

"Mom, I need the police," Monica managed to say.

"Monica, what's wrong?" Monica's mother asked, extremely concerned.

"Mom, Carlos isn't moving," Monica sobbed.

"Monica, stop crying. I can't understand you," her mother said.

"It's Carlos, Mom. He isn't moving. I keep calling his name. He won't answer. I need the police."

"Monica, I'm hanging up and dialing 911," Monica's mother told her, not completely sure what was going on but knowing something was seriously wrong.

"Hurry up, Mom, please," Monica pleaded as she leaned her back against the wall. She looked over at her husband's still and bloody body. She looked at her hands. They were cut up and smeared with blood as well. She dropped the phone, letting it dangle, bouncing off the wall. Slowly she slid down the wall to the floor, where she remained, scared to death, weeping, and screaming.

"CARLOS!"

Chapter 11

Angela stared out of the van's window, watching the busy early morning traffic. She was being transported to Norristown State Hospital to learn her fate. She smiled as she watched a group of teenage girls cross the street in their school uniforms. They reminded her of her own school days. Back when she and her now ex-husband were voted cutest couple and she and her friends were always joking around in class, cutting school and going to the mall, or participating in the school shows. Her happiest years were spent in high school, and she missed them dearly.

The driver pulled into the parking lot of the hospital. He and Angela entered the lobby and proceeded to the conference room where the hearing was to be held. The butterflies in her stomach were making her feel sick. She was praying to God every five seconds in her head. Please God, let Dr. Whitaker be here. Please let Ashley be on time. Please let them let me go.

The conference room was empty, with the exception of a young black guy dressed in a suit. He was sitting at the end of a long table, sipping coffee and reading a newspaper.

"Good morning," Angela greeted the unfamiliar man as she sat beside him.

The man said hello and continued what he was doing. Angela couldn't help peeking over his shoulder to catch a glimpse of the headlines. As she was scanning the paper, she came across an article about a woman who had almost stabbed her husband to death after finding out about an affair. Oh my God, Carlos? she thought to herself as she attempted to read the article thoroughly.

"Excuse me, sir, I don't mean to be invading your space or anything, but can I read that article right there?" Angela asked, pointing to the page. "If you're not reading it," she added.

"Oh sure," he answered, removing the page and giving it to Angela.

Angela's worst fear was confirmed: Carlos Vasquez, a Temple University aerobics instructor, is in critical condition in Frankford Torresdale Hospital, where he suffers from multiple stab wounds allegedly inflicted by his wife, Monica Vasquez.

Angela gasped. Her face froze, and she felt paralyzed. Within moments other people entered the room and took seats. Among them were an older white woman with short red hair, whom everyone referred to as master or judge; the doctor who had originally 302'd Angela; and Dr. Whitaker, who would act as Angela's public defender. Everybody greeted one another and greeted Angela as well. But she didn't respond to any of them. Instead, she stared into space.

"Ms. Williams?" Dr. Whitaker said, a concerned look on her face.

Angela shook her head as if she was snapping out of a trance. "Oh, I'm sorry. I was thinking about something."

"Are you all right?" asked the man who was reading the paper.

"Yes. I'm fine. We can start," Angela said hurriedly, still appearing zoned out.

The master looked at Angela strangely, and said, "Well, it looks like everyone is present, so we can begin. Doctor," the master said, gesturing toward the doctor who had committed Angela.

"Good morning," Dr. Wayne began. "Ms. Williams was brought to Frankford Torresdale's emergency room eight days ago, where I determined that she had attempted suicide. I based my analysis on the amount of Vicodin and alcohol that was found in her bloodstream. I believe that had she taken one more pill, she would have died, which is why I 302'd her."

"Frankford Torresdale, Frankford Torresdale, Frankford Torresdale," Angela mumbled.

The master looked over at Dr. Whitaker, who was sitting beside Angela. She shot Angela another strange look before she asked, "What have you observed from the patient, Doctor?"

Angela's foot began shaking under the table.

"Good morning, everyone," Dr. Whitaker began, trying to ignore Angela's distracting behavior. "In these past eight days since being admitted, Ms. Williams has not attempted suicide, she has not asked for any items that could be used for such an attempt, nor has she spoken of any such actions. She also has not shown any signs of depression and has been in a better mental state with every passing day. I advised her to start a diary as a way of expressing herself privately. She took my advice, and not only has she followed it, but she has shared with me how beneficial the method was for her. Based on our sessions and on reports from other staff members, it is determined that Ms. Williams is not a danger to herself or anyone else, and is capable of being placed back into society."

The master turned to the young black guy and asked, "What do you have for us today, Doctor?"

"Is the patient on meds?" the young man asked.

"Yes. I prescribed antidepressants," Dr. Whitaker responded, looking through Angela's chart.

"Well, she needs them now. Master, it's clear that the patient still requires treatment."

"That's not true," Angela said in her defense, again seeming to snap out of a trance. "You just want me to stay in Taylor's. It's your job to put me there. That's why you're here. What other purpose do you city solicitors serve? You're just a prosecutor with a doctorate. You don't know me. You haven't worked with me. You haven't seen how I've progressed. You're just here to make me look unstable so they can commit me. I'm not stupid."

Dr. Whitaker interrupted. "Ms. Williams, shh. You are making this very hard on yourself," she whispered to Angela.

Meanwhile, the master watched Angela closely.

"All I wanna do is get out of here!" Angela shouted with tears in her eyes. "Something has happened to somebody I love dearly, and I need to be by his side!"

Everybody grew perplexed, not knowing what Angela

was talking about. For all they knew, she was crazy and needed to be medicated.

"I don't think she's ready. Maybe a couple more months," the city solicitor suggested to the master.

"Ms. Williams, I'm committing you to another sixty days in Taylor's Institution for Behavioral Health," the master said.

"*Noooo!*" Angela sobbed. "Why are y'all doing this to me? Y'all want me to kill myself or something? Is that what y'all want?"

"Remove her, please," the master said, as she focused on signing some papers.

Dr. Whitaker sorrowfully patted Angela on her back. The driver who had brought Angela to the hearing forcefully escorted her out of the conference room.

"Ashley!" Angela screamed when she saw her sister waiting outside the room.

Ashley just stood in the hallway with tears in her eyes. She felt bad for her sister, but there was nothing she could do. Truthfully, she thought it was best for Angela to be detained. At least then she knew her sister was safe. Whenever Angela was out, it seemed Ashley was always on edge, worrying that every time the phone rang it was somebody with some bad news about her sister.

"They want me to kill myself!" Angela continued to scream as she was being restrained and taken out of the hospital.

Meanwhile, Dr. Whitaker joined Ashley in the hallway.

"I don't know what went wrong in there. Your sister was doing exceptionally well. I-I just don't understand," Dr. Whitaker said, vexed.

"I thought she would be getting discharged today. When I spoke to her, she said she had done real well and she was confident that she would be getting out. What happened?" Ashley asked.

"She just went blank. In the middle of the hearing, in front of the judge and the prosecutor, it was like she just blanked out. Then she verbally attacked the prosecutor and started mumbling things under her breath. I-I don't know. I'm as confused as you are. But, anyhow, they gave her sixty days," Dr. Whitaker said with pity. "I feel so bad for her. I mean, she really did try hard all week. She desperately wanted to get out today. She was determined not to get committed."

Ashley shook her head and said, "Some things are just out of our control. I just hope she gets better."

"That's the truth," Dr. Whitaker agreed. "Just keep in touch with her. Check in on her every chance you get. I'm sure she can use the support."

"I will," Ashley said, then she walked toward the elevator to leave the building.

Monica was sitting as far away as she could from the smelly homeless woman who was stretched out on the steel bench they had to share. Still in the dirty, blood-stained clothes from hours before, she felt disgusted. She was combing her fingers through her tangled hair when a heavyset black woman opened her cell.

"Monica Vasquez," the corrections officer said.

Monica stood up from the edge of the bench and followed the officer out of the cramped cell. She didn't know where she was headed, but she prayed it wasn't anywhere near the woman who had been going through withdrawal in another cell or the one who had been complaining loudly about the bloody tampon that was in the toilet stinking up her cell.

"Match your feet up with those footprints right there," the officer told Monica.

Monica did as she was told. She wanted to know what was going on but was too afraid to ask.

"Hold this under your chin," the officer said, giving Monica a piece of paper. "I'm gonna take a front shot and a side shot of you. Then you'll go over there and get fingerprinted."

Monica broke her silence. "Um, excuse me, what is this for?"

"You're being charged."

"Charged? Charged with what?"

The officer yelled to another officer, "She wanna know what she's bein' charged with."

"Attempted murder," the other officer yelled back.

Monica's heart dropped. She couldn't believe what she was hearing. "But, but . . . I didn't attempt to kill anybody," Monica said.

"Well, that's for the jury to decide, not us," the officer said as she snapped a picture. "Soon as you get done, you can make a phone call."

When they finished fingerprinting Monica, an officer escorted her to a pay phone.

"Mom," Monica said once her mother picked up.

"Oh, Monica, what are they saying?" Monica's mother asked, concerned.

"They charged me." Monica's voice cracked.

"With what?"

"Attempted murder," Monica struggled to say.

"Oh, Monica, sweetheart. It's all in the news. They're painting you as a monster. I have to keep changing the channel so the kids won't catch it," Monica's mother cried.

Monica broke down, "Mommy, what did I do? I didn't try to kill my husband. I didn't and I never would have wanted my kids to see a thing like that, Mommy."

"I know. I know. The minute they set bail, call me. I'm coming to get you, okay. I'm getting you out of there. We'll figure this out together."

"Mom, how is Carlos? Is he going to be okay?"

"He's in ICU. But the doctors said they were sure he would pull through."

"Oh, God," Monica wailed. "What about the boys? How are they holdin' up?"

"They would be fine if the damn police would leave them alone. They keep questioning them over and over. I had to tell them to get out of my house," she explained, still crying.

"Mom, what did I do to deserve this? I just tried to be a good person, Mommy. I just tried to be a good wife and a good mother. How did I mess that up?" Monica cried.

"Monica, you hold it together. You didn't do anything, you hear me? You just hold it together. I'll be there as soon as they set bail."

"Okay."

"I love you."

"I love you too, Mom."

Monica hung up. She returned to her holding cell, where she cried the whole time she was waiting for her turn to see the judge. She had never felt so much pain in her life. The thought of Carlos being in ICU without her by his side was killing her. Then there was the fact that her kids were in the middle of this big mess that she created, all over a woman. She didn't think she would ever be able to forgive herself for putting her family through so much over something so small and worthless. Her husband having an affair didn't call for all that, she thought. She was paying big-time for her mistakes, emotionally and soon to be financially after figuring lawyer fees. She wished she could turn back the hands of time.

Angela was strapped to a stretcher with her hands and feet bound securely when she was returned to Taylor's. The staff, including Vanessa, looked at her with shock. They didn't expect to see her return, let alone in restraints. Her face was pale, and her eyes were half closed. She looked exhausted, as if she were passed out. Her hair was no longer arranged neatly in a bob, but looked frizzed and disheveled. Her clothes were wrinkled. It looked as if she had been in a fight.

Vanessa was the first to go to admissions. "What happened?" she asked.

"They said she just snapped and went crazy at the hearing," an EMT told her. Vanessa followed procedures and reported the information she had gathered to the rest of the staff so they could prepare for Angela's stay. One staff member went to Angela's room to make sure there weren't any items there that Angela could possibly use to harm or kill herself. Another staff member went into the kitchen to get lunch out for Angela. Vanessa checked Angela's chart and prepared her meds.

Angela was taken to her room after being evaluated, searched, and given food and medicine. She had been cooperative, but in a puppet kind of way. It wasn't like before when she eagerly did what she was told. This time she just let the staff do whatever they wanted to her. She wasn't necessarily compliant, but she didn't refuse any procedures either. She was like a corpse being prepped for her funeral. When staff members searched her, she stood slumped over, putting no effort into helping them along. If they wanted her arms lifted, they had to lift them themselves. When it came time for her to eat, Vanessa fed her. The only things Angela did on her own were chew and swallow. Vanessa even put her medicine in her mouth for her and held a cup of water to her lips for her to drink. All the while, Angela never spoke a word. Her facial expression never changed. For the staff, the difference between Angela the day before at the cookout and Angela hours after her court appearance was like day and night. In their field it was quite a common occurrence. But for Angela, it was devastating. She had come so far just to end up right where she started, and this time it was over a man who wasn't even her husband.

It had been a long wait, but Monica was finally on the list to see the judge. She bit her nails nervously as she sat in front of the monitor.

"Pick up the phone, ladies," a corrections officer instructed Monica and two other women in the room.

"Hello," Monica said softly.

"Vasquez, Monica Vasquez?" the voice on the other end of the phone said.

"Yes."

"Verify your address, please."

Monica slowly recited her address.

"Birth date?"

"July 15, 1972."

"Okay, Ms. Vasquez, you understand you were charged with attempted murder . . ."

Monica sighed.

"Your record is clean, but under the circumstances, with there being children involved, we will not be able to grant bail for you—"

"What?" Monica cut the judge off.

"You'll remain in custody for the duration of your trial. Your preliminary hearing will be one month from today."

Monica was angry. She slammed the phone down and immediately started crying. The other two women in the room were giving her strange looks as the CO escorted her back to her cell. She wasn't even able to call her mom and tell her what had happened. The CO said she was too irate to be let out of the cell, which made her even madder. She lost control, screaming and cursing out the CO; kicking the bars, the walls, and the toilet. Eventually she crawled into a corner and started softly banging her head against the wall. Hurting and desperate for comfort, she shut her eyes in an effort to force herself to sleep.

Chapter 12

"Hi, I'm here to see my daughter, Monica Vasquez," Monica's mother stated as she approached a big counter inside PICC penitentiary on State Road.

"Let me see your ID, please," said the light-skinned woman behind the counter.

"Stand still. Don't move," Monica's mother said to Chris and C.J. as she let go of their hands to get her driver's license out of her purse.

The twins followed their grandmother's instructions and stood still beside her. Their big brown eyes looked around at the people in the waiting area and then up at the police officers behind the counter. They seemed scared but didn't say a word.

"Okay. Sign in here, and make sure you sign their names too," the woman told Monica's mother as she slid a clipboard across the counter. "Oh, and how old are they? Are they school-age?"

"Yes, they're five," Monica's mother answered.

"Well, you're not supposed to bring kids here during school hours."

"They're my daughter's sons."

"Still. That's policy. You can bring them here after school hours."

Monica's mother began to get frustrated. "Well, I didn't know that. I came all the way here to see my daughter. And these are her kids. She's looking forward to seeing them today. Can you make an exception, please?"

The woman looked over at the clock. It was two fifteen. "All right. This is what you can do. You can have a seat over there and at three thirty you can come up here and do the sign-in process again."

"Are you serious?" Monica's mother asked. "I have two five-year-olds with me. They're only in kindergarten, for Christ's sake. They're not missing anything, believe you me."

"Listen, that's not my rule, ma'am. Now I'm really working with you. Usually, you would have to leave and come back another day or go up without the kids."

Monica's mother rolled her eyes and took a deep breath. She fought back tears and swallowed her pride as she realized she had little choice in the matter.

"Okay," she said, then led her grandsons over to the waiting area.

"Knock, knock," Vanessa whispered as she slowly opened the door to Angela's room.

Angela was lying on her bed facing the wall, still in her nightclothes. She wasn't under the covers. In fact, the bed was neatly made. She was stiff. Her eyes were open and unblinking. The room was dark and cold and silent.

"Angela," Vanessa whispered as she stood in the

doorway. "I'm getting ready to leave. Do you need anything before I go?"

Angela didn't respond. She didn't even budge. Vanessa walked into the room and stood over her.

"How about you get out of your pajamas and take a warm bath? You may be able to get some sleep if you get comfortable," Vanessa suggested. "Where's that bubble bath stuff you like? I'll run the water for you."

Still there was no response from Angela. If it weren't for her stomach moving up and down, Vanessa would have thought she wasn't breathing.

"Ms. An-ge-la," Vanessa sang softly. "I'm trying to help you out. You know once I leave nobody'll be back in here to check on you. So you better tell me if you need anything now."

Vanessa was trying everything to get Angela to talk to her. It had been over a month, and she still didn't know the whole story of why Angela had been sent back to the institution in the first place. But whatever the reason, she knew it was getting the best of Angela. She knew how bad Angela wanted to get out and how hard she had tried to make that happen. She knew Angela was crushed, and she felt sorry for her.

"It's two fifty-eight, Ms. Angela," Vanessa warned. "My shift ends in two minutes. I won't be back until tomorrow. You better tell me what you need. Something to drink? Anything?"

Angela said nothing.

"All right. Well, I'll see you tomorrow. Good-bye," Vanessa said as she slowly left Angela's room.

* * *

It was a quarter after five by the time Monica's mother and sons were able to see Monica. She came into the visiting room wearing a red jumpsuit. Her hair was braided in the back, and she appeared to have lost weight. She lit up, though, when she saw her mom and the two boys.

"Heeey!" Monica squealed as she squeezed her sons tight. Chris and C.J. just grinned bashfully. They still didn't quite understand what was going on.

"Aw, look at my baby," Monica's mother said, breaking into tears.

Monica rubbed her mom on the back. "Mom, don't cry. You're gonna make me cry," she said. "I need you to be strong for me."

Monica's mother wiped her tears and looked up at her daughter. "Monica, I can't help it," she said, shaking her head from side to side. "I didn't expect it to be this bad. Do you know what we all had to go through to get to this point? They checked my bra. They made Chris and C.J. open their mouths and take off their shoes." She broke into tears again. "This is no place for you. This is no place for your sons to visit you," she cried.

Monica rubbed her mom's back again while wiping her own tears. It hurt her to hear what her sons had to go through to see her. She missed them so much, but she didn't know if she could stand having them visit her in jail again.

"I'm sorry, Monica," Monica's mother said, wiping her face with a napkin. "I didn't mean to get so emotional on you. It's just that—"

"I know, Mom. You don't have to say it. Well, anyway, look at my babies. You two got big since the last time I saw you," Monica said to change the mood.

"Didn't they," Monica's mother agreed. "They can eat too. I swear, I've been food shopping three times and it's only been a little over a month," she joked.

"You don't have to tell me," Monica said.

"So . . . what now?" Monica's mother asked. "So much for that preliminary hearing. You didn't get to say a word," she added.

"Yeah, well, my lawyer told me it would be that way. Now we have to wait another month for the trial," Monica said, her eyes again filling with tears. "Mommy, what did I do?" Monica began to sob. "I just tried to be the best wife I could be. How did this happen? How did my life just spin out of control like this?"

Chris and C.J. grew sad watching their mother break down. They started crying with Monica, and that hurt Monica to the core. She couldn't take it anymore. She wound up ending the visit early, even though in her heart she wanted it to last forever. The truth was, it pained her too much to be in the emotional state she was in around her sons.

"Mom, I'm sorry, but I have to let y'all go. I can't take it. I can't sit here and let my babies see me like this. I thought I would be able to handle it, but . . ." Monica wept.

"Say no more," Monica's mother said as tears fell down her own face. She gave Monica another hug and kissed her on the cheek. Then she held her daughter's face in her hands and said, "Monica, baby, everything is going to be all right. God is going to see us all through this one.

And that woman? God help her soul because if I ever cross paths with her, she's going to wish she never kept a diary."

Monica sucked up her tears and bent down to give her sons one last hug and kiss before painfully watching them leave the visiting room.

"Mom-my!" her sons cried out as their grandmother took their hands and led them out of the room.

The walk back to her cell was dreadful for Monica. Her sons screaming *Mommy* played over and over again in her mind. She felt guilty for ending the visit early. She wondered if she was a bad mother for not spending every minute she could with her kids. She didn't know. She was an emotional mess. Once in her cell, she collapsed onto her bunk. She cried herself to sleep as usual. It was her only means of relief.

Chapter 13

"There were multiple stab wounds in the chest, neck, and left arm," a forty-something male said as he sat in the witness stand beside the judge.

"How many is multiple?" the prosecutor asked, approaching the witness.

"Twenty-two."

"No further questions, Your Honor," the prosecutor said.

"Would you like to cross-examine?" the judge asked the defense attorney, barely concealing his disinterest.

"No, thank you, Your Honor," Carnell Lucas replied.

"You may step down, Doctor." The judge nodded toward the witness.

"Call your next witness," the judge ordered the defense.

"I'd like to call Monica Vasquez to the stand," said Carnell Lucas.

Monica stood up from her chair next to her attorney. She glanced back at her mother, who sat anxiously among the other spectators. Monica's frail and shaky body treaded to the witness stand, where she was sworn in. Feeling insecure and intimidated, she took the seat beneath the judge. The judge was a man, sure to be sympathetic toward her husband and disgusted with her, she thought. She feared for her freedom. All she could think about was spending the rest of her life in prison and having to be without her children. Her heart was beating a hundred times faster than normal. She was nervous and hated to have to take the stand, but her attorney strongly advised it. He was known for being sharp, and he had a good reputation, so she followed his lead without question.

"Mrs. Vasquez, how long have you and your husband been married?" Lucas began.

"Ten years," Monica answered.

"How had you planned to spend your ten-year anniversary?"

"Aside from the week we spent in Florida, I planned a surprise dinner at the restaurant where he proposed to me."

"What happened to those plans?" Lucas asked as he glanced over at the jury.

"Well, the day we got back from Florida I found out a lot about my husband."

"Elaborate, would you please, Mrs. Vasquez."

Monica took a breath. "I found out that he had been having an affair for four years and that he had been living a lie all along."

"How did that information make you feel?"

"Devastated . . . betrayed."

"What did you do?"

"I left and went to a friend's house," Monica reported.

"And when did you return home?"

Monica looked up at the ceiling as she tried to remember back to that night, close to two months before. "It was between midnight and one o'clock in the morning," she replied.

"Why did you decide to go home at that hour?"

"I intended to stay the night at my friend's, but while I was there, I found out that she and my husband had slept together as well. At that point I couldn't stand to be in her presence. I just wanted to be with my children, somewhere away from the both of them." Tears began to form in Monica's eyes as she relived the pain she felt that night.

"When you say the both of them, you're referring to whom?"

"My husband and my friend."

"So you left your friend's and went home?"

"Yes."

"What did you do once you got home?"

"I woke up my kids and put them in the car."

"What was your husband doing when you got home?"

"He was sleeping on the couch."

"In what position was he sleeping?"

"He was on his back."

"Did you at any time while he was sleeping come into contact with him?"

"No. I tried to hurry out before he could wake up."

"Why?"

"Because I didn't want to have to confront him. I just wanted to be with my kids, alone, somewhere where I could clear my head."

"When did you make contact with your husband?"

"He woke up right when I was leaving the house."

"What did he do when he woke up?"

Monica looked up at the ceiling again. She wanted her story to be accurate.

"He called my name. I believe he asked me what I was doing."

"What happened next?"

"Well, I told him I was leaving and taking the kids to my mom's. But he didn't want us to go."

"Did he try to stop you?"

"Yes. He did stop me."

"How did you end up in the kitchen?"

"He took the car keys from me, and he went in the kitchen to get a drink of water," Monica explained, wiping a tear from one eye. "I followed him in there to get the keys back. I told him I wanted to leave. I told him that I had found out about him and my friend and I couldn't be there with him. So he threw the car keys at me."

"Did the keys hit you or did they fall to the ground?"

"They hit me."

"Where did they hit you?"

"Right here," Monica said, as she pointed to her nose.

"What did you do after the keys hit you in your face?"

"I remember running at him and knocking him down."

"Then what?"

Monica paused and then responded, "I remember the water jug fell on the floor. I remember hearing the glass break. Then I remember being on top of him punching him."

121

"You were punching your husband with a closed fist or open?"

"Closed. I was just punching him. I was upset. I had a lot of anger inside."

"When did you pick up the piece of glass?"

Monica shook her head and replied, "I don't remember picking up a piece of glass. It wasn't until I saw cuts on my hand that I realized I had a piece of glass in my hand."

The tears that Monica fought hard to hold back came pouring from her eyes. Her attorney handed her a tissue and waited for her to pull herself together.

"While you were stabbing your husband, were you or were you not conscious?"

"I was conscious, but not conscious of what I was doing," Monica said.

"What do you mean, Mrs. Vasquez, and please, take your time," Lucas said, then he took a few steps back.

"I mean"—Monica sniffed—"I had no idea I was stabbing him. I thought I was just punching him. I don't even remember seeing any blood until after it was all done."

"What did you do after you realized your husband had been stabbed?"

"I remember getting my kids and looking for the phone to call the police."

"When the police arrived at your home, what did you tell them?"

"I told them my husband was bleeding and that he wasn't moving," Monica recalled, dabbing her eyes again with the tissue.

"Did you tell them that you stabbed him?"

"No."

"What did you tell them happened to your husband?"

"I just told them he was bleeding."

"Why didn't you tell them that you had stabbed your husband?"

Monica's shoulders rose as the palms of her hands turned faceup. She replied, "Because I didn't believe I had stabbed him. I was out of it. I didn't know what had happened."

"No further questions, Your Honor," Lucas concluded, as he subtly winked one eye at Monica and returned to his seat.

Monica wiped her eyes again as the judge permitted the prosecution to cross-examine. The process was grueling for Monica. The prosecutor made her look guilty. He drilled her with confusing questions: Is it true that after reading parts of the diary you told your best friend you were going to kill your husband? You really didn't intend to take your children to your mother's house at one o'clock in the morning, correct? Instead, you used that explanation as an excuse to go home and confront your husband, didn't you? He painted a picture of Monica that was the exact opposite of her true character. After answering the prosecutor's questions for seven minutes, which felt more like seven hours to Monica, she was back in her chair at the defense table. The judge called a brief recess while both sides prepared to do their closing statements.

Monica sat still and quiet, trying to keep her racing mind intact. She was still on edge about the whole diary thing and her husband's affair. Now she had a trial and a verdict to worry about, adding insult to injury. It was a wonder she didn't have a nervous breakdown. But it was the sole thought of her children that motivated her to maintain her sanity. She was determined to be strong for them. They were her heart and the only reason she had to get through the tragic situation she found herself in.

Bells from a church could be heard in the distance. The courtroom was filling up as people were returning from cigarette and bathroom breaks and others from a brief lunch. Monica and her lawyer were exchanging words as the time for closing arguments was drawing near.

"All rise," the bailiff said as the judge reentered the courtroom.

The group of spectators, family, and media rose from their seats, as did Monica and her attorney.

"Commonwealth, the floor is yours," the judge said, giving the prosecution its chance to take center stage.

The prosecutor stood up and took his position. His hands were folded, and his elbows rested on top of the podium.

"Your Honor and the jury," he began, "we all know how it is to be in love with someone, to be head over heels for a person, to idolize someone and hold him on a pedestal where he is deemed perfect, angelic, and can do no wrong. And we also know how painful it can be when that person does something to crush those ideals, forcing us out of the fantasy we once were in and bringing us into the reality we've avoided for so long. When the trust is taken away and the perfection is flawed. When we

learn that the person we so truly and dearly loved has betrayed us in a rather hurtful manner, in, perhaps, the
most hurtful manner. I've heard it described as a broken
heart, a crushed heart, or even a stolen heart. And we all
know what it's like to want revenge on the person who
has broken our heart or crushed it or stolen it. And by
definition revenge is payback, or getting even, which
means we may want to break, crush, or steal that person's heart as he did ours. But is it literal? In our minds,
whether we are emotionally tainted by the dishonesty
and infidelity we've been forced to confront, do we think
to act on our feelings in such a literal way?

"Well, in this case, yes. The defendant, Monica
Vasquez, did in fact seek revenge in a literal way. She did
break, crush, and steal her husband's heart, and she did
so with a six-inch-long, two-inch-wide piece of glass. A
piece of glass, ladies and gentlemen, that could not alone
have cut through her husband's two hundred thirty
pounds of lean muscle. That piece of glass was sharp
enough to have punctured a man's physically fit chest
only with the assistance of a strong and mighty arm.
Mrs. Vasquez forcefully and fiercely struck her husband,
the victim, Carlos Vasquez, with all her might to cause
the damage she did. Not only did she use such force, but
she also knew exactly where to strike her husband.

"In the heat of anger and even in complete disarray,
we as human beings, as creatures with consciences and
emotions like guilt and love and sorrow, we know when
enough is enough. We know when to stop while we're
ahead. We know that stabbing someone in a vital organ
repeatedly and repulsively can injure him badly, if not

murder him. So we tend not to go that far. We tend to stop while we're ahead, unless," the prosecutor said, as he raised his finger and his voice simultaneously. "Unless we intended to do just that—*murder*," he concluded. Slowly he scanned the jury's faces, then took his seat.

Monica swallowed hard as she felt her heart beating through her blazer and blouse. The prosecutor's closing statement had her second-guessing her own innocence, so she could imagine what questions it brought to the minds of the jurors.

"I rest my case, Your Honor," the prosecutor said once seated. He took a sip from the glass of water that sat in front of him, and he sneered over at Monica.

"Defense," the judge said, giving Lucas the floor.

Carnell Lucas approached the podium. He put on his glasses and then began to speak.

"Your Honor, ladies and gentlemen of the jury," he said, addressing the court. "Monica Vasquez is a young woman, mother of twin boys, a preschool teacher. She's educated, respectable, well liked—the typical American citizen, no different than you or I. She just happened to encounter a chain of unfortunate and unforeseen events that turned her ordinary life into an extraordinary one. Like many other people, including ourselves, possibly, Monica Vasquez has experienced a tragedy in which she and her husband are both victims, not to mention their children.

"Now, you've heard the testimony of several people during this trial. You've heard from the professionals and the experts. You've heard from the prosecution, and myself, but you hadn't heard anything until you heard from

Monica herself. She told you all you need to know to make your decision in this case. She told you she and her husband had just come back from a week's vacation celebrating their ten-year wedding anniversary. She told you that in addition to that, she had made dinner reservations for the two of them at one of their favorite restaurants. Then she told you the news that abruptly ended her happy state in her marriage. Imagine receiving a diary at your home and in it reading some awful truths about the person you vowed to spend the rest of your life with. Further imagine seeking refuge from a best friend, who has been like family to you for years, and learning that your friend has betrayed your trust as well. Where does one go from there? Who does one turn to for love and consoling? For Monica, it was her children, the only people who could offer her the peace and comfort she desperately needed at the time. So she went home to get them. She just wanted to hold them in her arms and be with them through the night. She told you that she saw her husband sleeping on the couch when she walked in the door and that she quietly walked straight up the stairs and got her children out of bed. She walked back downstairs and directed her children to go to the car. All while her husband slept. It wasn't until he woke up and caught her getting ready to leave that she confronted him. In fact, she told you she didn't want to have to confront him at that time. She had tried, though unsuccessfully, to get in and out of the house quickly and quietly without waking her husband. In her own words, she told you she did not intend to hurt or murder anyone. If, ladies and gentlemen of the jury, Monica Vasquez was seeking revenge, as the prosecution has suggested, if she wanted to literally break her husband's heart, wouldn't she have done so while he was lying on his back asleep, harmless and vulnerable? Wouldn't she have gone into the kitchen and grabbed a knife, a large knife, one that would really do the job? Why would she wake her children first and attempt to leave her home? Why would she walk past her sleeping husband several times without even doing the slightest thing such as nudging him or even slapping him if she was so angry?

"Because, ladies and gentlemen, it's simple. Monica Vasquez did *not* intend to badly injure or kill her husband. She didn't even intend to argue with him that night. But, as we all know, some things in life don't always go as we intend. And this is the case at hand. Monica Vasquez found herself in a position that went extremely out of the way of her intentions. She found herself caught up in a bad accident. A temporary state of incompetence, unconsciousness, mental letdown. She wasn't herself at the moment. She wasn't aware at the moment. She wasn't alert at that moment. All we know is that she was present at the moment. A moment, a brief moment that would change her life forever. A moment that she would come to regret instantaneously. A moment she will have to carry with her throughout her life. A moment during which she did harm her husband. But a moment she definitely did not intend!

"Your Honor, I rest my case."

Chapter 14

Taylor's was quiet for a Saturday afternoon. A few residents sat in the lounge playing checkers, reading, and talking among themselves. The television was on, but no one was watching it. Three of the four staff members on duty were in the office watching the residents through the Plexiglas. The fourth staff member was sitting in the lounge area with the patients. Vanessa was inside her station with her door open. She was doing a crossword puzzle.

"Monica Vasquez was found guilty of attempted murder yesterday after stabbing her husband repeatedly when she found out about his long-term affair after reading a diary sent to her by his mistress. She could face ten to twenty years in a women's maximum-security prison. Her attorney had this to say . . ." a woman's voice droned on from the television speakers.

Vanessa stopped what she was doing and turned her attention to the TV screen. Monica Vasquez, she thought. Why does that sound familiar? Vanessa put her crossword puzzle down and locked up the medicine cabinets. She left her station and walked down the hall to Angela's room.

Angela was in her bathroom vomiting when Vanessa knocked on her door.

"Angela, it's Vanessa."

"Here I come," Angela called out as she wiped her mouth with a washcloth. She flushed her toilet and opened her door. It was two o'clock in the afternoon, and again she was in her pajamas. Her hair was all over her head. The polish on her nails was chipped, and her hands looked rough and ashy.

"Oh, Angela, this isn't like you," Vanessa said, looking her over. "You have got to get it together, hon. This has been going on too long now. What is it? What's bothering you?"

Angela shook her head as if to say nothing, then suddenly ran back into her bathroom. She had to vomit again.

Vanessa sat on Angela's bed, and her eyes scanned the room. She wanted to make sure there were no harmful items around.

"Are you okay?" Vanessa shouted out.

The toilet flushed, the water ran, and Angela was out of the bathroom once more.

"Angela, is there anything you wanna talk to me about? You have been moping around here for a couple of months now. And they're planing to up your meds. And you know what that means. They up your meds, they lengthen your time. Now, I suggest you get whatever it is on your chest off because that's the only way you'll start making some improvements around here."

Angela rested her head in her hands. She didn't say anything, but she wanted to. Vanessa was right. There was something weighing on her, tearing her down, and it was something much bigger than her losing control and acting out of character at court and being hit with sixty days.

Vanessa asked, "Is it Vasquez?"

Angela lifted her head out of her hands and looked at Vanessa in amazement.

Vanessa continued, "I saw it on the news. Angela, you told me you were sending that diary to a friend."

Angela eyes widened. "What did you see on the news?"

"The woman, Monica Vasquez, who you had me mail that diary to. They said she tried to kill her husband over that diary, and now she's goin' to jail for ten to twenty years behind it all," Vanessa explained.

Tears immediately gathered in Angela's eyes. "Did they say whether or not he was all right?"

"Who? The husband?" Vanessa asked.

"Yeah. Carlos."

"They didn't say. Well, then again, I wouldn't know 'cause as soon as I heard her name and realized where I recognized it from, I stopped watching and came down here. Now you need to tell me what's going on," Vanessa demanded.

Tears fell from Angela's eyes. "Vanessa, I messed up. I messed up so bad."

"You can talk to me, Angela," Vanessa said in a comforting tone.

"Vanessa, you have to swear on your life you won't say anything to anybody."

"I cross my heart and hope to die," Vanessa said, making a cross with her fingers.

Angela took a deep breath and wiped her tears. She turned to face Vanessa and began, "Back in August of 2000, shortly after my divorce, I signed up for a body-toning class. Carlos Vasquez was my instructor. Well, I was attracted to him right away, but it was nothing serious. Besides, I was there to relieve stress, not retrieve it. Getting involved with another man was the last thing on my mind. But we took a liking to each other. We connected. Brief conversations after class led to lunches and even dinners. He was so articulate when it came to physical fitness. He had every aspect of it covered, and so I would go to him for tips—workout tips. Then as time passed I started turning to Carlos for advice . . . you know, about men and things that were going on in my personal life.

"It was early November, I told Carlos all my business. He had an hour before his next class, and I had called off work, so we decided to have brunch at this diner called Silk City. I don't know what it was about that day that made me feel the need to pour my heart out to Carlos. I remember it like it was yesterday."

"*My divorce took a lot out of me. I'm a changed girl since. I'm messing with a married man, David. I guess it's my way of getting even with my ex and his mistress,*" *I told Carlos as I took a breath.* "*But every time I'm with David, I'm reminded of all the things my husband did behind my back while we were married, and it makes me sick,*" *I said.* "*I find myself spending yet another night taking straight shots of Jack Daniel's and popping Vicodin after Vicodin. Then the next thing I know, I'm in Taylor's seeing a shrink and taking meds.*"

"Taylor's? What's that?" Carlos asked.

I looked down in embarrassment. I didn't know if I should have shared so much information with him. I didn't want to scare him away. But after all, he was a friend, and, hell, I had no one else to confide in.

"A behavioral health . . . well, a mental institution," I said, cutting through the bullshit.

Carlos's eyebrows rose. "You would never strike me as someone who had been in a mental institution before," he said.

"Well, try three times in the last year." I shook my head and sipped my hot chocolate. "My husband really messed me up. But every day gets better, especially now that I'm taking your class. My last doctor told me it would be a good idea to work out—you know, to divert the negative energy, to relieve all the stress and tension."

"Yeah, that's true. Working out is beneficial for many things," Carlos said, nodding his head in agreement.

"Just that small talk alone had left me feeling so free. I felt like a burden had been lifted off of my shoulders. I had found someone I could talk to about anything, and it felt good.

"My class with Carlos ended too quickly, in my opinion. So I signed up for his January through May class. We had gotten a whole lot closer over those next four months. He began to confide in me as well. He told me everything, everything about his wife and kids. Every day it was something about them—sometimes good, sometimes bad—but they were all he ever talked about.

"He told me when his wife got sick, when his mom died, when he caught crabs at the gym and accidentally gave them to his wife and sons. He was devastated about that. It took him forever to forgive himself, even though he hadn't done anything wrong. He loved the hell out of his family. He told me about the time he went to San Diego for two months to do a workout video. He told me about the time he lied to his wife about having to work because he didn't want to go to her family reunion in Texas. He was being spiteful because she never wanted to go to Florida to see his mom. He told me everything. We were real friends. We had exchanged numbers and everything. We called each other only when necessary, though, and it was agreed upon that I would call him only during business hours, never too late at night, you know, out of respect for his wife. I found myself signing up for all his classes. Months soon turned into years, and they were good years, you know. I hadn't attempted suicide, and I hadn't been in here since I met Carlos—well, up until now. But as far as I was concerned, anyone who could keep me out of this place was to be cherished. He was probably my only reason for living at one point. I mean, I credited him with saving my life. Shoot, once he really did save my life.

"One day I called Carlos before he left for his evening class. I was going through something with David that had to be straightened out, and I was going to be late for class."

"I'm coming to tonight's class, but I'll be a little late," I told Carlos over the phone.

"All right. I'll see you when you get there, but don't be too late. We're going to be learning some good stuff," Carlos said.

"Well, I probably won't be able to do any new exercises. I'll tell you about that later—after I meet with David this evening."

"Is everything all right?" Carlos asked, his voice filled with concern.

"For now," I told him. *"I'll talk to you about it when I see you."*

"That could have been the last time I ever spoke to Carlos. That night David met me at my apartment. Dealing with him, I got caught up and wound up getting pregnant. Of course David wanted me to get an abortion, and it wasn't because he was afraid his wife would find out. He just didn't want to pay child support. I didn't want to get an abortion. First of all, I don't believe in them, and second, I wasn't about to get rid of a baby just because his trifling ass didn't want to pay for it.

"We got into a big argument over the whole thing. The next thing I knew, I was being choked to death. Right before I felt myself passing out, my phone rang. It was Carlos. He had left a message: *'Hey, it's me, I'm ending class early tonight. My wife called, and one of my sons has a fever, so I'm going home. I'll talk to you tomorrow. Hope everything went well during your meeting with David.'*

"David immediately loosened his grip. I guess he was smart enough to figure out that if he did kill me, it would get out that he was the last person I was with and he would eventually get caught. He gave me a disgusted look while I was gasping for air, like he didn't just try to kill me. Then, without saying a word, he just got up and left. I was thankful for Carlos's wife that night. If she hadn't called Carlos and asked him to come home, he wouldn't have called me and left that message, and I probably wouldn't be here to talk about this.

"Anyway, I decided to keep the baby. For six months I stayed clear of Carlos. I was big and pregnant, and I didn't want him to see me like that. I had the baby in April 2003. It was a girl. I named her Carla Sabrina and I gave her up for adoption. That was the hardest thing I had to do in my life. I never told anybody about it. I was ashamed. I just got back to my life. I contacted Carlos and started his classes again. He was like my savior. Everything got better whenever I was with him. I was falling for him, but I kept my feelings to myself. I respected his marriage and the fact that he was so in love with his wife. I really did.

"But one day after class he was telling me about a surprise he was planning for his wife. Their ten-year anniversary was coming up, and he wanted to do something extra-special. He was planning to rent a beachfront villa on Marco Island for them to stay a week. He even wanted to rent a limousine to pick them up from the airport and take them to the island. I suggested a stretch Porsche. Then out of nowhere, I blurted out, 'I wish my name was Monica.' I realized my mistake when Carlos looked at me funny. I could tell he was uncomfortable, probably even offended. From then on he started distancing himself. Slowly but surely, the lunches stopped. The long talks after class got shorter, and I knew I was losing him. I was hurt. I wanted things to go back to the way they were, so I asked if we could meet one day and talk. After hesitating, he told me yeah. So I took off work and pumped myself up to tell him exactly how I felt. I wanted him so bad, and I'm not talking about as a friend. I wanted him to be my man, my significant other. I knew he was married and happy, but it's been almost four years that we've been friends—going out, talking, confiding in each other, and mind you, he hadn't told his wife a single thing about me. He told me he didn't want her to worry about something that was nothing. But I thought it was something. You know how you can tell when somebody likes you? I thought that he was just scared to step out on his wife. At least that's the type of vibe I got from him. But now when I think back, it could have just been me wanting him that bad that gave me those vibes. I fell for him hard, Vanessa.

"He was supposed to call me and let me know where we could meet. It was supposed to be early in the afternoon. Well, he never called, and when I finally called him, he treated me like I was just some strange chick off the street, like I was a nobody. He cursed me out. He had an attitude and everything. He acted like he barely knew me, like we never had a friendship or anything. I was hurt. I started thinking about all the bullshit my husband put me through. I started thinking about David and my baby. I felt betrayed for some reason. Like Carlos had let me down. Like all the drama I had been through was all his fault. I really felt like he had broke my heart. I remember opening the bottle of Merlot that I had bought specifically for our meeting, and I remember getting the Vicodin from the medicine cabinet. After that, all I remember is my sister coming to my house with the police. Next thing I know, here I was again, staring at these bright walls and lights. Doing the meds, seeing the doctors, and listening to the staff thing all over again. I was devastated, Vanessa.

"Do you know how it feels to believe you are well and then find yourself sick again, starting over from scratch to rebuild happiness that took so long to gain? I was fed up with being miserable and getting the short end of the stick all the time. I was desperate to get that happiness back again. So when Dr. Whitaker suggested I start a diary, something clicked in my head. I thought I had the perfect plan to win Carlos back. And really I just wanted his friendship back—at the least. But I knew there would have to be some friction between him and Monica before he would give me the time of day again. So I made up the diary. Well, actually, I just replaced David's name with Carlos's and used all the information I got from Carlos over the years to make it sound believable."

Vanessa kept quiet, in part because she was at a loss for words and also because she didn't want to say anything that would discourage Angela from confiding in her again. She just sat quietly and nodded understandingly at Angela.

"I had you send it to his wife. But I thought she would just leave him. I figured he would need a shoulder to cry on or somebody to talk to, and I would be right there. And possibly we could have become a couple, but truthfully, I would have been happy just being friends again. I never meant for it to come to this. When I saw that article in the newspaper about him almost being killed, I lost it. That's why they committed me again. I lost it in front of everybody. Because I knew that it was my fault.

"He could be dead because of me, Vanessa." Angela began to cry. "And now his wife is about to spend all those years in jail, away from him and away from their children. He's really going to hate me now. I am hopeless. I did all this to get him, and all I did was make matters worse. I know how much he loved his wife and his family. And I took that away from him. There is no way in hell he will ever want anything to do with me after this. What was I thinking? Vanessa, I feel so sick with myself. Ever since I found out the consequences of what I did, I haven't been able to eat or sleep. I'm always throwing up. God works in mysterious ways, though. Because if I would have never seen that article before court, they would have discharged me, and I swear, the minute I found out what had happened to Carlos, I would have killed myself."

Vanessa let out a breath as she processed all of what Angela had confessed. "Oh, boy, Angela, that's a lot to digest," she said, breaking her silence. "I mean, if I had known this beforehand, I would not have put that diary in the mail."

"Vanessa, I didn't just tell you all of that for you to start feeling guilty," Angela said.

"Well, I don't know what you expect from me. I mean, this woman's life is in shambles now, and I had a part to play in it."

"Vanessa, you only acted as a friend. I was the one who messed up. Not you. I deceived you just like I deceived Monica. I have to live with this, not you," Angela explained, continuing to cry.

Vanessa shook her head in disgust. "Angela, I'm glad you're still here. You really do need help, and I pray that one day you get it," Vanessa said, and she stood up and walked out of Angela's room.

Monica was sitting on a prison bus staring out the gate-covered windows. She was in an orange jumpsuit, and her wrists were in handcuffs. She was being transferred from PICC to Muncy prison upstate. She was trying with all she had to keep from crying, but it was extremely hard. She could not believe her fate. Her entire life had changed instantly. She flashed back to the Marco Island trip she and Carlos had taken just a couple short months earlier. If someone had told her then that she would be headed to jail to serve a ten- to twenty-year sentence for almost killing her husband she would have just laughed. Now, here she was in shackles, on a prison bus with two armed policemen watching her and the other women like dogs. Her children would grow up without their mother. Her husband was in the hospital fighting for his life without his wife. And an entire public knew Monica Vasquez as a jealous wife who tried to kill her husband over an affair. How could this be? Monica thought. What did I do to deserve this? Monica was dying on the inside as she tried to make sense of the tragedy that hit her family.

When the bus arrived at Muncy, the inmates were let off the bus and led into the facility. They were stripped to nothing and searched systematically. First, Monica had to lift each of her breasts. Then she had to spread her butt cheeks and vagina. Last, a female guard had to rummage around in Monica's hair piece by piece. After that humiliation, she re-dressed and was taken to her cell.

A female corrections officer walked Monica down the block. Inmates were staring at her as she passed by them. Some shouted things.

"CO! Bring 'er in here!"

"Oh, that's a prima donna right there!"

Monica felt so many emotions, it was a wonder she didn't have a nervous breakdown. She was scared to death, first of all. She wasn't the fighting type and barely ever got in confrontations with people. She knew she was no match for any of the women in that prison. She didn't belong there, among the most dangerous of criminals. In addition, she was still dealing with everything that had been going on with her family. It wasn't like she committed a crime that had nothing to do with her husband and kids so that they could go on with their regular lives. Her family was destroyed, and there was no one to hold it together. Her children were without both their parents. And even though her mother was her children's support system, there was no one to be there for her mother. It was killing her every time she thought about the grand scheme of things.

Monica and the CO approached the tiny cell. There was a woman on the top bunk asleep. The CO unlocked the cell and let Monica inside. Once in the cell, the CO removed the handcuffs from Monica's wrists, left the cell, and locked the big, thick iron bars. Monica sat down on the bottom bunk. Her face fell into the palms of her hands, and all the tears she had fought to hold back came rushing out at once. She began sobbing uncontrollably.

"Shut the fuck up! I'm tryna sleep!" Monica's cellmate shouted.

That was merely the beginning of Monica's nightmare. She saw no way out as she quieted herself and silently prayed to God, asking for a miracle.

Chapter 15

"MAIL!" a correctional officer shouted to the block of inmates. Hands started to appear through the thick iron bars. Monica stood up from her bunk and approached the CO.

"Bless you," she said as she collected her mail.

Receiving letters and pictures from her mom and her sons had been Monica's only means of maintaining her sanity while she had been in the county prison for the past three months. Now that she was upstate awaiting her sentence, she definitely needed to hear from her family. Being incarcerated with hundreds of women who had murdered and robbed people took a lot out of Monica. Seeing women be killed and raped in the prison was enough to make her lose her mind. And then there was the way the COs treated her and the other inmates like animals, feeding them food that resembled garbage, talking to them disrespectfully, and ignoring their personal well-being.

After Monica took her mail she sat back down on her bunk. Her face lit up as she noticed the return address on the first envelope. It was from her sons.

She opened the letter eagerly and silently giggled at the stick-figure pictures of her family they had drawn. She read the subtitles that, in a five-year-old's handwriting, read: Mommy, Daddy, Grandma, C.J., and Chris. She couldn't help but laugh at Chris's oversized head on the drawing. She knew that C.J. must have been the artist. She opened a second envelope. Inside was a Christmas card from her mother, wishing her happy holidays. Inside the card was a letter telling her to be strong and to keep her faith in God.

A third envelope from a Vanessa Cooke took Monica by surprise. She set it aside, afraid to open mail from someone she didn't know or expect to hear from. The last time she had done that, she wound up losing her best friend and almost her husband all in the same night. She decided against opening it as she pushed herself farther back onto her bed, allowing her back to rest against the hard, cold wall. She ran her fingers through her unkempt hair, untangling it along the way. A tear fell from her eye. She was an emotional mess dealing with so much at once. She picked up the drawing her son made for her and stared at it, laughing and crying at the same time.

"What the hell's the matter with you?"

Monica covered her mouth and forced herself to stop crying.

"I'm sorry, Annette, I didn't mean to wake you," Monica said to her cellmate with a cracking voice.

"You know I sleeps through da mail. You couldn't wait 'til chow to start dat cryin' shit?" Annette asked, all attitude as she repositioned herself on the top bunk.

Monica stood up from her bunk. She figured she would try to make Annette feel better by offering her the letter she received from the unfamiliar woman.

"You want some mail?" Monica asked.

"Why? You got some for me?" Annette asked back.

"Here, it's yours," Monica said as she handed over the unopened envelope.

Annette snatched the envelope and read the front.

"Dis is for you, not me," Annette said huffily, handing the envelope back to Monica. "Man, got me thinkin' I had some mail," she added.

"Pretend it's for you. I don't mind," Monica said.

Annette sat up lazily. "Give it here," she said with a grin, her lips twitching.

Monica handed Annette the envelope once more.

"Fuck you, Mom. Fuck you, Dad. Fuck you, family. I got my own mail!" Annette sang out loud.

Monica smiled and watched Annette open the letter.

Annette had been locked up for most of her young life and had been in that particular prison for a little over two years. She was serving time for several counts of vehicular homicide. She had been only nineteen years old and high on angel dust when she ran a stolen car going seventy miles per hour into the back of a minivan on a residential street. Every passenger in the van died, including a seven-month-old girl.

"Read it out loud," Monica said, pretending to share Annette's excitement about having mail.

"Damn, you wanna hear all my business," Annette said, this time only pretending to have an attitude.

"Come on," Monica said. "Please."

"All right." Annette sighed as she unfolded the letter, then playfully cleared her throat.

" 'Dear Monica Vasquez,' " Annette began. "Naw, fuck dat. Dear Annette Leanne Roberts," Annette said jokingly.

Monica just chuckled.

" 'You don't know me. My name is Vanessa Cooke. I'm a nurse at the institution where Angela Williams was placed. I want to start off by saying I'm sorry about your husband and what has happened to you and your family. I heard about your case on the news. It got my attention because your name sounded so familiar. Then it dawned on me that I was the one who sent you the diary. Well, let me rephrase that. I was asked by Angela to mail the diary to you, but she said that it was being sent to a friend as a way of her opening up and getting things off her chest without actually talking about them.

" 'Anyway, Angela confided in me some months back that she did not have an affair with your husband. In fact, nothing in the diary was true, well, nothing that was said about your husband. She made it all up because she was obsessed with Carlos, who was nothing more to her than a fitness instructor and friend. Angela is mentally unstable, especially when it comes to men, and that is part of the reason why she did something so stupid and cruel. I feel extremely bad for you, which is why I'm bothering to write. Ever since Angela confessed to me what she had done, and being I'm the one who put the diary in the mail, I haven't been able to stop thinking about you and your family. It took me so long to say anything because of my job's confidentiality agreement. I didn't want to get fired. But now that Angela has been recently discharged, I am able to speak about this.

" 'I don't know the law too much, but I'm sure if you speak to your lawyers about this, they can find a way to appeal and maybe get you out of there. You know, because Angela purposely misled you. Maybe you can use this letter as evidence. Or maybe you need me to testify. I will. I feel so bad that I mailed you the diary. Had I known what it was really about, I would have never sent it for Angela. I'm sorry for Angela's behavior, and I'm sorry you had to go through all you did for nothing but a lie. Sincerely, Vanessa Cooke,' " Annette finished reading, then refolded the letter.

Monica's face was blank as she tried to register what she'd just heard.

Annette slid the letter back in its envelope and handed it to Monica. "I think you might wanna keep dis one. Thanks anyway," she said.

Monica reached out and accepted the letter, her expression still blank. "I don't believe it. This woman is still fucking with me," Monica said.

"I don't know, man," Annette said. "This sounds official."

"No, no, it's her. I bet you it's her. She wants me to go crazy. She wants me to lose my mind. Seeing that I almost killed my husband wasn't enough. Seeing me go to jail wasn't enough," Monica said, shaking her head.

"Let me see it again," Annette said, holding her hand out.

Monica passed the envelope back to her.

"If it was her, she wouldn't have put her return address on here," Annette said, looking at the front of the envelope.

Monica looked at the envelope, paying heed to what Annette was saying. "So, wait a minute. She's saying I went off for nothing. That . . . that I fought my best friend and almost killed my husband and put my children through all this bullshit for nothing! That I'm here getting ready to spend the next ten to twenty years of my life in prison for no reason at all. No. *No!*" Monica said, gasping with disbelief.

Monica backed away from the bunk beds while the words in the letter sank in. Pressed against the wall, she held her face in her hands. "I MESSED UP MY WHOLE LIFE FOR NOTHING! FOR SOME CRAZY, LUNATIC BITCH! NO! NO! THAT'S BULLSHIT! TELL ME IT'S BULLSHIT! TELL ME ALL THIS IS JUST A DREAM! JUST ONE BIG FUCKING NIGHTMARE! PLEASE! OH GOD! OH GOD!" she cried in anguish.

Monica was trembling. The pain she felt now was more overwhelming than any pain she felt since the day she read the diary. She could not believe that this was happening to her. It seemed like just yesterday her children were at her mother's eating hamburgers and hot dogs and playing their video games. Wasn't it just yesterday when her life had been as normal as the next person's? She never could have imagined going through the turmoil that she had in a few short months. Never in a million years did she see herself being locked up in prison facing ten years minimum for almost killing her husband, the man of her dreams, a man she loved wholeheartedly and who had loved her the same. They'd had the perfect life and family, and now it was all lost—for nothing, for absolutely nothing. She was crushed. There were no words to describe how she felt. Nothing could measure up. Dying would have been better at that point.

The fresh snow that covered the streets and the Christmas lights that decorated the houses made Christmas Eve look perfect. Angela was one of the few people out and about. She was doing some last-minute food shopping. She had decided to cook dinner and spend the holidays inside alone. Ashley had invited her to join her at her boyfriend's house, but Angela didn't want to be up under a couple. She didn't need anything reminding her of how badly she wanted a companion. If she went to Ashley's boyfriend's and watched them cuddle and say sweet things to each other the whole evening, she was sure she would end up back at her apartment drinking a whole bottle of wine and popping pills, so she declined.

It had been a little over a month since Angela left Taylor's, and she was determined to keep it that way. She made sure to take her meds every day on time, and she even participated in outpatient therapy sessions. The Sunday following her discharge she went to a neighborhood church and got baptized. She asked God for forgiveness for all her wrongs and even said a prayer for Monica and her family. She hadn't attempted to contact Carlos in any way, although she paid close attention to the news just in case they mentioned any changes or updates about him. She was concerned about his recovery. There wasn't a day that went by that Angela didn't regret sending the made-up diary to Carlos's wife. But her medication helped her live with the regret.

Angela paid for her items and left the supermarket. She loaded her bags in her car and quickly got inside. After she started the car, she put her hands over the vents to get the chill off them, then drove to her apartment.

"My turkey is in the oven. Now I can take me a nice long bath," Angela said to herself as she poured a glass of sparkling water and left the kitchen. In her bedroom Angela put on Carl Thomas's CD. She hummed along to "Summer Rain" as she lit candles in her bathroom and ran a bubble bath. As she waited for the tub to fill, she pulled out a pair of panties and a bra from a drawer and placed them on her queen-size sleigh bed. She then retrieved a negligee from her closet, which she placed neatly beside her underwear. Back inside the bathroom, the water was ready. Angela turned out the lights and stepped into the tub.

"Oh, this feels so good," Angela mumbled as she lay her head back on her bath pillow. Between the warm bath, the refreshing glass of sparkling water, the smell of the turkey cooking, and the sound of Carl Thomas, Angela was in heaven. For the first time in years, it hadn't taken a man to put her there.

Chapter 16

"Merry Christmas, Mommy!" C.J. shouted through the phone.

"Merry Christmas, baby," Monica moaned. "I miss you so much. Did Santa Claus bring you everything you asked for?"

"Yeah! I got a PlayStation and some games! I got my bike with no training wheels! Some clothes. A tent thing—"

"Oh wow, it sounds like you been a good boy then, huh?"

"Chris got the same thing too. But his bike is blue. Mine is black. Oh, Mommy, I got a surprise for you." C.J. was excited.

"You do?"

"Yeah, hold on."

"Merry Christmas, Monica," Carlos said, then burst into tears.

Monica almost dropped the phone. She hadn't expected to hear her husband's voice.

"Carlos?"

"Baby, I love you so much. It's breaking my heart that you're in there. I can't live without you," Carlos cried.

"Carlos, you're okay? I've been thinking about you every day. I am so sorry, Carlos. I never meant to hurt you and our sons like this," Monica cried.

"I know, baby, I know. We're goin' to get you out of there, you hear me?"

"My mom told you about the letter?"

"Yes. I could kill that woman, Monica!" Carlos said with anger.

"Why did this have to happen to us, Carlos? Everything was perfect with us," Monica cried. "I'm in here with these women, and it's hell, Carlos. The way they look at me, how they talk to me, it's like I'm constantly looking over my shoulder. Then having to eat and sleep at specific times. It's crazy in here. I don't belong in a place like this."

"I know. Just hang in there. You won't be in there much longer. Your mom was talking to the lawyer all morning. He's going to ask the judge to have leniency, you know, because of the letter not being able to be admitted into evidence," Carlos said.

"Well, we'll see. I don't want to get my hopes up. But what about you? How are you holding up?"

"Better. I'm staying at your mom's now with the boys. I'm just worried about you now. When I finally heard what happened and realized the extent of everything, with you being found guilty and facing so much time, I-I couldn't . . ." Carlos again began to choke up.

"It all happened so fast. I didn't know how to react to everything. I'm still trying to put all the pieces together. Especially now, after getting that letter that said it was all a lie. Carlos, I feel so stupid. I should have known better.

I should have known you wouldn't do anything like that. I should have trusted you," Monica continued to explain.

"It wasn't all your fault, Monica. I had my part to play in this too. All I had to do was tell you about Angela. The minute I found out how she really felt about me and I ended our friendship, I should have told you about it. I know you would've understood, and when you got that damn diary you would have known what it was. You would have known she was just trying to be spiteful. And all this could've been avoided," Carlos said.

"We both made our mistakes, but the one who should feel guilty is her!" Monica said angrily. "She destroyed our whole lives behind this bullshit." Tears re-formed in Monica's eyes.

Carlos immediately tried to uplift his wife. "Well, after they sentence you, the lawyer said he'll put in a request to appeal. He's confident the conviction can be overturned."

"Carlos, baby, I hope he's right. I don't know how much longer I can do this," Monica cried.

"Baby, now that I'm out of the hospital, I'm doing everything in my power to get you out. I love you, Monica. You are my wife, the love of my life. You shouldn't be in nobody's prison." Carlos cried with his wife.

"Well, Carlos, that's my time," Monica said as she glanced up at a CO, who was giving her the eye. "Give my mom and the boys kisses for me."

"Okay. I love you, Monica," Carlos said quickly.

"I love you too, Carlos."

Chapter 17

Angela was asleep on her couch when the phone rang. She turned over and picked up the cordless that was lying on the floor. With a raspy voice she answered, "Hello."

"Hey, sis, you 'sleep?" Ashley asked.

"Oh, hi, Ashley. Yeah, I was knocked out. What time is it?"

"A little after nine. What, you had a late night?" Ashley asked, her tone filled with suspicion. Ever since Angela had been home, Ashley been checking on her, and any time Angela sounded off, overslept, or didn't want to be bothered, Ashley couldn't help but wonder if she'd fallen back into a depression. That was one of the reasons Ashley preferred Angela to be in Taylor's.

Angela sighed and responded, "No, actually, I went to bed early last night. I just forgot to set my alarm."

"Well, are you going to work today?"

"Yeah. I'm about to drag my butt out this bed."

"Well, I'll call you later to check on you. And don't forget, I have a plate here for you."

"From Christmas? Girl, please, you might as well throw that out."

"It was only four days ago. I froze it."

"No, thank you."

Ashley sucked her teeth and said, "Well, I'll eat it then, shit."

"No offense. I just had so much of my own food left over from Christmas. I'm tired of turkey and macaroni and cheese."

"Oh. Well, go get ready for work. You're already late," Ashley said, ending their chat.

"Okay. Thanks for calling and checking on me."

"No problem. Talk to you later."

"All right. 'Bye."

Angela pressed the end button on her phone and let it drop to the floor. Her television was still on from the night before. The news was on, but the volume was turned down. Angela started feeling around for the remote.

"I wonder what the weather is going to be," she mumbled to herself as she turned the TV up.

"A bizarre turn of events leaves Monica Vasquez just days away from freedom. Vasquez was tried and convicted of attempted murder after having stabbed her husband nearly to death back in September. She would have had to serve a minimum of ten years, but it looks like she'll be out after having served only three months. According to a letter Vasquez received while in prison, the supposed mistress of her husband, Carlos Vasquez, was not his mistress at all. Instead, she was just a student of his who had become obsessed with him and had fabricated a diary to cause turmoil in his marriage. This information, along with a petition started by Carlos Vasquez himself, led the judge to overturning Monica Vasquez's conviction. She'll be returned to the county until the proper paperwork is received, then released. Police are not providing any details regarding the deranged woman who made up the diary that began this whole ordeal, except that she has been in and out of mental institutions following her own divorce. It's been a roller-coaster ride for Vasquez and her family, who are relieved at the outcome."

"Well, I'll be damned!" Angela said. "That damn Vanessa!"

Angela sat up on the couch and reached down to grab the phone again. She dialed some numbers.

"Hello, can you connect me to Vanessa Cooke?" Angela asked with attitude.

"Hello, this is Vanessa," Vanessa's voice cheerfully greeted Angela.

"Vanessa, it's Angela."

"Angela, how are you?"

"Vanessa, I told you not to say anything about that diary situation, and you go and write her a letter all about it. What's up with that?" Angela said straight out.

"Angela . . ." Vanessa was caught off guard. She didn't know what to say. For one, she was at work, which was not the appropriate place for her to get into it with Angela.

"Don't you know you can lose your job for that? Isn't that like a part of your confidentiality code, not to discuss shit that your patients told you? If I can't trust a motherfucker at Taylor's, who the hell can I trust? That's the *one* place I'm supposed to be able to pour my guts out to people, and the minute I do, shit like this happens. And y'all expect a motherfucker to get better. I was doing good!"

"Angela—" Vanessa tried to butt in.

"I was doin' so good!" Angela continued, not letting Vanessa speak. "I spent Christmas by myself, all alone eatin' a big-ass home-cooked meal at the table by myself, and not once did I take a pill or sip some wine. I didn't even cry, Vanessa. As bad as I wanted to, I told myself that it would only lead to me feeling sorry for myself and wanting to take my life. So I fought those tears. Because I was determined to turn over a new leaf! But every time I think I'm doing good, somebody throws salt in my game!"

"Angela, I didn't mean for it to hurt you in any way," Vanessa managed to squeeze in.

"WELL, WHAT THE FUCK DID YOU DO IT FOR? NOW, THEY TALKIN' ABOUT ME ON THE NEWS AS SOME DERANGED WOMAN WHO BEEN IN AND OUT OF MENTAL INSTITUTIONS!"

"They're not allowed to mention your name," Vanessa said, remaining calm for the sake of the patients and staff just outside her office.

"SO WHAT DOES THAT MEAN?"

"Nobody knows who they're talking about."

"I DO! YOU THINK I NEED TO BE REMINDED THAT I'M A DERANGED MENTAL PATIENT WHEN I TURN ON THE NEWS?"

Vanessa huffed and said, "Angela, I will talk to you later about this. I really didn't mean any harm. I just couldn't keep something like that in. It was really eating at me. I'm sorry."

"VANESSA, DO YOU NOT UNDERSTAND? THEM DAMN NEWSPEOPLE ARE GOING TO DIG AND PRY UNTIL THEY FIND OUT WHO I AM, AND I'M GOING TO LOOK UP AND IT'S GOING TO BE CAMERAS EVERYWHERE. THE MINUTE I WALK OUT MY DOOR. AT MY JOB!"

"I can't talk about this right now. I really can't," Vanessa said, then hung up.

Angela heard the click and grew more irate. She felt a migraine coming on as she started flicking through the channels, turning on every news broadcast. As she suspected, each one talked about the Monica Vasquez case and the crazy woman who lied about being her husband's mistress. She started pacing her apartment. Angela was furious. The last time she was that angry was the day Carlos had stood her up. Much like that day, she started having flashbacks to other times when people had hurt her. Her migraine kicked in, and she was losing her ability to cope with the pain she was feeling both physically and mentally. It wasn't long before she was running to her medicine cabinet.

She dialed numbers on the phone again.

"Vanessa Cooke, please."

"This is Vanessa," Vanessa said, slightly annoyed.

"I'ma kill myself, bitch, and it'll be on your watch. Now, how will *that* eat at you?"

Click.

Monica's body looked frail stretched out across her bunk. She had a box in one hand, and with the other she was snatching Christmas cards and drawings down off the concrete wall. She smiled as she took down pictures of her children and placed them neatly in the box. She came across the last of her wall décor and then stopped. She stood up.

"Come down here and give me a hug," Monica said, looking up at Annette, who had been lying on her bunk reading a book.

Annette hesitated at first, and then she put the book aside and leaned over toward Monica. With tears in her eyes she extended her arms out and brought Monica into her.

"I'm going to miss you too, Annette," Monica said.

"I wish I was walkin' out dis bitch behind ju," Annette said, squeezing Monica tight.

"I wish you were too," Monica replied sincerely.

The two of them had gotten close during the course of time they had been cellmates. Monica had become a mother figure to Annette. And Annette looked out for Monica in her own way. Even though she had an attitude with Monica all the time and came off rude to her, she made sure no other inmates messed with Monica. She vouched for her in the prison.

"I'll write you all the time," Monica said as she pulled away from Annette. "You won't be wanting to sleep through mail again," she added.

Annette's face lit up, but only for a moment.

"Dat's wassup," Annette said, letting go of Monica.

"Let's go, Vasquez," the CO called out.

Monica left the prison cell and proceeded down the

corridor accompanied by two correctional officers. She didn't smile, even though her insides were glowing. She didn't want to upset the other inmates. She was doing something some of them would never do—she was getting out.

Chapter 18

Monica's case had been the talk of the nation. It had been aired on all the major news broadcasts and printed in all the major newspapers. There were cameras and reporters everywhere outside the county prison on the day of her release.

"Mrs. Vasquez, how does it feel to be free? Mrs. Vasquez, what would you say to the woman who sent you the false diary? Are you nervous about seeing your husband?" were just a few of the questions Monica dodged before she reached her car.

Carlos was in the driver's seat when Monica got in. They fell into each other's arms instantly. Cameras flickering and all, they sat in the car hugging for minutes before they finally drove away.

"Oh God, thank you, thank you, thank you," Monica said as she squeezed Carlos's free hand. "There's so much I have to do today. I have to go to Rita's and thank her for writing me back and accepting my apology. Then I have to go see my dad. All I thought about was what if he passed while I was in there," Monica said as tears gathered in her eyes. "And then we can go to my mom's.

I think I want us all to spend the night there with her. I just want us all to be together my first night out."

"Anything you want," Carlos said, freeing his hand from his wife's hold and using it to wipe a tear from her eye. "But first, we have to talk about this," he added, pulling a bunch of mail from the glove compartment while keeping his other hand on the steering wheel.

"What's all this?" Monica asked.

"Publishers have been sending all kinds of mail. They told your mom they want to write your story, and wait until you see how much of an advance they're offering," Carlos told Monica with a smile.

Monica began opening the mail and skimming the pages.

"Oh my God, for real? Five hundred thousand dollars?" Monica said, holding her hand over her mouth.

"So, what do you think?" Carlos asked, bouncing his eyes back and forth between Monica and the road.

"I-I don't know. This is so sudden. Why didn't you and Mom tell me sooner? When did you first hear about this?"

"Your mom thought it would be best to wait until you were out," Carlos explained.

Monica let out a scream, and she and Carlos both chuckled.

"Well?" Carlos asked.

Monica took a deep breath. "Well, it could give me a chance to set some facts straight. And God knows we could use the money. What do *you* think?" She turned to her husband.

Carlos glanced at Monica and answered, "The whole

thing is already out in the public. So I say, Why not. You never know where it can take you."

"Well, that's it. I'll do it!" Monica said, wiping tears of joy from her face.

A half-hour later Carlos and Monica pulled onto Rita's street and parked right behind her Jeep. Monica anxiously waited for Rita to open the door after she rang the bell.

"Arrrhh!" Rita screamed, happy to see Monica.

Monica threw herself into Rita's arms, and the two of them hugged. Again, Monica started crying tears of joy.

"Rita, you are truly a friend. On some of those days you were the only one who kept me going with those silly jokes you wrote me. Thank you so much for forgiving me."

Rita shook her head and said, "That's what friends are for. You were going through some hard shit. And it wasn't your fault. You were misled."

"That's why I love you," Monica said.

"Aww, I love you too," Rita said, hugging Monica again. "I'm so glad you're home. I know the twins must have flipped out when they saw you."

"They haven't seen me yet," Monica corrected Rita. "I came here first."

"What? Girl, you better get on home to your boys."

"I know. I'm going. I just had to come see you first. Once I get with them, that's it. I won't be seeing anybody for a few days," Monica explained.

"I know that's right. Well, I'll be by there to see you after you spend some time with the family."

"All right, Rita," Monica said, heading back to the car.

"See you," Rita said, waving to Monica.

Carlos beeped the horn as he and Monica drove off.

Next, Monica went to see her father in the nursing home where he stayed. He didn't really comprehend Monica's ordeal due to his suffering from Alzheimer's. But Monica wasn't expecting anything from him during her visit anyway. She just wanted to see him and tell him that she loved him.

After making their stops, Carlos and Monica reached Monica's mom's house just in time for dinner. One of Monica's favorite dishes was waiting for her, spaghetti with shrimp, crabmeat, and Italian sausage in the sauce.

"Oh, Mom," Monica gasped as she ran into her mother's arms.

"Mom-my!" Chris and C.J. shouted together, and they ran out of the kitchen toward Monica.

Monica immediately broke down in tears as she dropped to her knees and grabbed her sons.

"Oh, babies, Mommy missed you so much," she cried. "I am so sorry you had to go through so much. I promise I will make it up to you. If it takes the rest of my life, I will make sure you two end up all right. You hear me? Mommy is *so* sorry. You hear me? I never meant to hurt you or your father. And your daddy and me are going to be just fine. Just fine."

Carlos and Monica's mother stood together weeping as they watched Monica hold the twins. Meanwhile, Monica continued to talk to her boys, kissing them on their heads and faces.

Monica didn't want to let her sons go. Even during dinner one sat on each of her legs. She was overwhelmed emotionally, finally able to experience the unconditional love of her kids.

Chapter 19

Monica was sitting on her front steps watching her sons shoot hoops in their driveway. It was a nice June day, and she was enjoying the weather, but she couldn't wait for Rita to arrive so they could be on their way to her first book signing. She eagerly watched every car that turned the corner, praying it was her best friend. Finally, Rita's red Jeep appeared.

"Chris and C.J., come on. Aunt Rita's here. Mommy's about to go," Monica said as she stood up.

"Hi, boys!" Rita yelled as she pulled into Monica's driveway. "Monica, sorry I'm late. That damn sister of mine wouldn't let me off the phone."

"It's okay," Monica said as she led the twins inside.

"Gimme kiss," Monica said, holding her cheek out toward her sons.

"Oh, Ma," they said, kissing their mother's cheeks simultaneously.

"Honey, Rita's here!" Monica shouted as she grabbed her pocketbook off the couch and headed out the front door. "You and the kids be there in about an hour, okay!" she added.

"We'll be there, don't worry. Just go, you're running late!" Carlos yelled from the bathroom.

"All right, I'm leaving! Love you! See you later!" Monica said before she walked out the door.

"How you got me late to my own book signing?" Monica asked sarcastically.

"I'm sorry," Rita whined playfully.

Rita backed out of Monica's driveway, and the two of them were on their way downtown.

"I can't believe all of this," Monica said as she fixed her hair in the passenger's-side mirror. "Who would have ever thought something so bad would turn into something so good," she added.

"Well, be blessed," Rita said, her eyes glued to the traffic.

"Oh, I'm definitely blessed," Monica confirmed. "I was ten seconds away from losing my husband and then was about to have to spend the rest of my life in prison behind it. And fighting with you like that. It was all so crazy," Monica babbled. "And I'm still so sorry for that," she added.

"Don't worry about it. It ain't like you whipped my ass," Rita said.

"I did whip ya ass," Monica said.

"What fight was you watchin'? I whipped ya ass," Rita corrected her.

"I whipped ya ass," Monica shot back.

"Bitch, please," Rita said, refusing to give up.

"Oh, a mailbox, pull over," Monica said, pausing their little spat.

Rita abruptly pulled her Jeep over and maneuvered it along the curb.

"We don't have time for stopping. We're late as it is," Rita just had to say.

Monica ignored her friend. She pulled a letter addressed to her old cellmate, Annette, from her pocketbook and stepped out of the car. She jogged briskly to the mailbox, dropped the letter in the slot, and returned to the passenger seat.

When Rita and Monica arrived at the book signing in the Gallery, it was packed. There was a long line of people, mostly women, waiting with their books in hand. Some were munching on refreshments. Others were chatting with one another while the rest just stood quietly, looking around the mall.

"Have a seat right here, Mrs. Vasquez," the event promoter said as he quickly pulled out Monica's chair.

Monica sat down and got comfortable. She put on a big smile as she prepared to sign autographs. This was her moment, and she knew she would savor it forever.

"Move, got damnit! Oh! God, these people can't drive!" Angela shouted as she zipped through traffic. "They act like they don't have anywhere to go!"

"Your love's got me lookin' so crazy right now. Your touch got me hopin' you page me right now."

Angela heard her cell phone's ring tone and slowed down.

"Oh, shit, that's where my phone's been all this time," she said to herself as she reached down on the side of the passenger seat to retrieve the ringing phone.

"Yes," Angela answered, loud and agitated.

"Angela, where have you been? I have been calling

you for like a month! You had me scared to death!" Ashley blurted out.

"I left my phone in my car," Angela said nonchalantly.

"I been callin' your house too. I have been driving past there like every week for the last four weeks. Everybody is worried about you. Your job called me. You haven't been to work. Apparently you threatened to kill yourself to somebody at Taylor's, and they been to your house. They're lookin' for you," Ashley gave her sister the rundown. "What's goin' on with you?"

"Ash, please. Taylor's can kiss my ass! They don't give a damn about me! They just want the five thousand a month they get to fill a bed in that motherfucker!"

"You're talkin' crazy."

"Yeah, well. What do you expect from a crazy person?" Angela asked Ashley. "Move, bitch!" Angela shouted at a double-parked vehicle.

"Angie, where are you? I'm coming to get you," Ashley said, concerned.

"No, no, no," Angela said, frustrated. "I'm tired of you always rescuing me. I'm sick of being a burden on you. I'm sick of being a burden on everybody. Just leave me alone. I'll be fine. Now, I'm tryin' to get somewhere if you don't mind."

"Angie, I'm your sister, and I'm worried about you. You're not in your right mind just now, and you don't need to be driving anywhere. Tell me where you are so I can come get you," Ashley pleaded.

"Why? So you can take me to Taylor's. No! I'm almost at the Gallery anyway. Save your gas!"

Click.

* * *

"Hi, how are you?" Monica said with a smile.

The short Caucasian woman smiled back with tears in her eyes, and said, "Hi. I just want to tell you that I admire your strength. You give women like me hope. I'm a new mother of twins, and I was going through some rough times recently, with postpartum and all, and I really was ready to give up. And when I heard your story it really opened my eyes. I realized how blessed I was. To see you be so strong after all you been through, it really picked me up. I imagined myself in your shoes and pictured me being locked away, not able to see my kids grow up, and it changed my perspective. I could never see myself without my children. Thank you so much for showing me that. I was really at the end of my rope," the woman said as she placed her copy of Monica's book on the table.

Monica opened the book and asked "What's your name?"

"Patty," the woman responded, teary-eyed. Monica signed the book and gave it back to the woman. Then she placed her hands over the woman's, and said, "God gave me that strength, and God gave my story to you so that you could get strength in your time of need. I'm so happy that God is working through me. And I'm so happy I could help you."

The woman dabbed at her eyes with a crumpled piece of tissue. She thanked Monica once again and walked away. Another woman stepped up.

"I'm so happy for you. I'm glad justice prevailed. God is with you," a young thirty-something woman said as she placed her book down on the table.

"Thank you so much," Monica said with warmth, and she opened to the title page.

"Kelly, K-E-L-L-Y," the woman said.

Monica scribbled some thanks and brief kind words on the page, then closed the book. She gave it to the woman, still smiling, and then greeted the next person.

"Hello," Monica said cheerfully.

"Hi," another young woman said as she approached Monica.

The woman put her book down on the table.

"Could you sign it to 'Angela' and write it with this?" the woman said as she scrambled through her purse.

Monica got goose bumps hearing the woman's name. Then, seeing a small black gun in the woman's purse, her heart skipped a beat.

"Angela Williams," the woman said as she pulled the .38 revolver from her purse and pointed it at her own temple.

Monica placed one of her hands over her heart and the other over her mouth as she gasped. The crowd of people dispersed, some running, some slowly walking away, others ducking. Rita was frozen in her chair.

"Don't do it," Monica managed to say before the gun went off.

A loud boom echoed through the busy mall. Shortly after, screams could be heard. Angela was stretched out on the freshly buffed floor. A puddle of blood immediately formed adjacent to her head. Sirens and police radios were heard in the distance. The media arrived within minutes. Everything was happening so fast, but to Monica, everything appeared to be moving in slow motion, yet in a blur.

Diary of a Mistress

* * *

"As if it weren't a bestseller already, there is more to Monica Vasquez's story. The alleged stalker and once-thought-to-be mistress of Carlos Vasquez showed up to Monica Vasquez's book signing today armed with a .38 revolver. She only made time to reveal her name before pulling the trigger and shooting herself in the head. She was pronounced dead at the scene.

"According to police, she left a short suicide note inside her copy of Monica Vasquez's *The Diary of a Mistress*, which simply said, 'Tell my daughter I always wanted her.' No one else was harmed in the mall this afternoon.

"It's been an ongoing tragedy for Vasquez, and she had only this to say: 'I'm just glad my children weren't here to see it.' "

Chapter 20

Monica and Carlos sat on their porch swing, watching the sunset and wrapped in each other's arms. It was early September and pretty warm outside.

"So, you think you can handle getting in front of a classroom again?" Carlos asked, stroking his wife's hair with his fingers.

"I think so," Monica said as she exhaled. "I think it'll be good for me. Getting back to my normal life, doing what I was doing before all the craziness," she added.

"Well," Carlos said, as he gently lifted his wife's head off his chest, "I'm going inside to get the kids ready for bed."

"All right," Monica said.

Carlos kissed his wife on her forehead, and said, "Happy anniversary, honey."

Tears came to Monica's eyes as she thought about the fact that she almost lost her husband that exact day a year earlier.

"Happy anniversary," she said, then returned her husband's kiss.

"Don't stay out too long, you have a big day ahead of

you," he concluded and he reached for the cane that was leaning against the wall near him.

"I'm right behind you," Monica said, not moving a muscle.

Instead, she sat there on the swing staring into the orange and pinkish sky, absorbing the beauty of the day, treasuring it as if it were to be the last one she'd live to see. She picked up her yellow notepad and opened it to a clean page. She retrieved the pen that was in between some pages and began to write.

Chapter 21

Monica pulled into her parking spot reluctantly and looked up at the big stone building. She smiled at the fall decorations that covered the small windows. There was an aura around the school that she didn't recognize. She felt somewhat out of place. She contemplated putting her car in reverse and going back to her comfort zone, her home. She had become a prisoner in her own house after the whole ordeal at her book signing. The only time she left was to go to the supermarket or to the dry cleaner. Other than that, she had spent most of the past few months inside. It was the only place she felt secure, protected from the stares and the whispers she had come to expect.

"Here we go," Monica said to herself as she took a deep breath.

She grabbed her pocketbook from the passenger's-side seat. She took one last glance at herself in her rearview mirror, then she stepped out of her car. She walked the ten feet to the entrance of the school and went inside.

Everything looked different inside the elementary school where Monica taught. It had been a long time since she'd been there for one, plus having gone through so much and spending time in prison, everything looked different to her.

"Hey, Mrs. Vasquez, welcome back." The secretary in the main office greeted Monica with a smile as she walked in to retrieve her mail.

Monica smiled back and said, "How are you, Ms. Crane, and thanks for welcoming me, I need it."

"Oh, you'll be fine. The kids are still as sweet as they wanna be. You'll see," the secretary said.

"That's good to hear," Monica said, retrieving a handful of papers and envelopes from her cubbylike mailbox.

"The only thing that has changed is the day. Other than that, everything here is the same," the secretary assured Monica.

"Yeah? Well, I'll see you later, Ms. Crane," Monica said, politely ending their small talk.

Monica walked out of the office and proceeded down a long hallway. Pictures of students and their achievements covered the walls. Announcements and a calendar listing events were stapled to a big bulletin board, and seasonal decorations bordered everything.

Sounds of children chattering in various classrooms could be heard throughout the halls. Teachers were scattered about, some holding conversations in the doorways of their classrooms, others settling their pupils. Monica was making her way to her room, taking her time getting there while she mentally prepared herself for her first day back in so long. It wasn't teaching that worried her. It was facing the children that made her uncomfortable. Having two young kids herself, she knew how brutally honest school-age children could be. Her biggest fear was that one of her students would ask her if she was the lady on the news who had tried to kill her husband.

Through the door's window that exposed the class she was assigned to teach, Monica could see an older woman sitting on a stool in front of a group of students. The children seemed to be very well behaved, quiet, and attentive to the elderly woman who sat before them. After another deep breath, Monica turned the doorknob and walked inside the class.

"Good morning," the woman said as she turned toward Monica.

"Hello," Monica said, forcing a big smile.

"You must be Mrs. Vasquez. I'm Mrs. Conner," the woman said, standing to shake Monica's hand.

"Well, it's a pleasure to meet you, Mrs. Conner," Monica said, forcing another smile.

"Don't worry, this is the best group you can have," Mrs. Conner said to Monica, sensing her nervousness.

"Children, this is your teacher, Mrs. Vasquez. Say hello and show her how we welcome our new teachers," Mrs. Conner slowly instructed the group.

The group of about nine preschoolers rose to their feet and darted toward Monica. They all gathered around her, wrapping their little arms around her legs and waist, almost knocking her off her feet. She was startled but pleasantly surprised. She appreciated them.

"Good morning, Mrs. Vasquez," the children sang.

Monica was pleased. The children had lifted her spirits and she was beginning to regain confidence. She hugged the children back, as many as she could, and they returned to their seats on the colorful ABC-123 rug.

"Okay, boys and girls, Mrs. Conner is going to leave you with Mrs. Vasquez now." The sixty-something lady spoke cheerfully in third person.

Mrs. Conner glanced at Monica and winked. She smiled and left the classroom. Monica was on her own. But she felt good about it, thanks to the good group of kids and Mrs. Conner's friendly welcome.

She sat in her chair at her desk and pulled the roll book from a desk drawer. She called the names of the preschoolers as they individually raised their hands to let her know they were present.

"Jamie Thomas, Maria Thompson, Shawn Walker," Monica called out, pausing in between to write in her roll book after each name. As she was approaching the end of the names, Monica came across one that sounded familiar.

"Carla Williams," Monica called out as she looked out at the group of children.

"Here," a tiny voice responded.

Monica looked at the girl, almost staring. She was so pretty and innocent. Monica couldn't help but wonder if she was the same Carla Williams Angela had given up for adoption. But before she found herself getting caught up in her thoughts, she just closed her eyes and silently prayed to God. God, please just continue to work through me. If this is yet another task you need me to complete, I'm yours.

Monica opened her eyes and took a deep breath. As she closed the roll book, a sudden calm came over her. She felt like a burden had been lifted off of her. She was ready to live again.

177

Acknowledgments

All praises be to Allah. Thank you for mapping this entire journey out for me. As Oprah Winfrey said once, "God will dream up bigger dreams for you than you will ever dream up for yourself." And this is so true.

To the readers, retailers, book clubs, and vendors: you all are my biggest support system. Without you, my writing would be purposeless. Thanks for embracing me.

Rich, you are my backbone. Thanks for being right there beside me through everything. I couldn't have made it without you. Love you.

Amir, your independence is a blessing because it allows me to do what I have to do. I am so fortunate to have you in my life. Allah made you perfect for me. I love you. Ooh Ma.

Mommy and Daddy, you two make me proud. You've come so far and I'm thankful that you both are here with me to share in my happiness. It wouldn't have been the same without you. Keep doing what you're doing. I love you both.

Blair, Qur'an, Whop, Tyree, Shamara, and Tiara: thanks for promoting me and putting your sister out there. Y'all know I love y'all.

Acknowledgments

Aunt Wanda and Uncle Jimmy, thank you once again. You two are always available and ready to help with any and everything. I can't thank you enough for that. Love you.

Aunt Netta and Uncle David, I owe you a lot for helping with Amir. Traveling is so much easier knowing my baby is in good hands. Thank you with love.

Uncle Neil and Dwayne, thanks for providing my New York home. It comes in handy with those high hotel costs. Plus, y'all have much more hospitality—home-cooked meals and a car. You can't beat that! Love y'all.

Aunt Merrie and Uncle Blake, just knowing that if I ever need you I can call on you without hesitation is a blessing. Many people don't have that. I appreciate you two with all my heart.

Aunt Debbie and Uncle Wayne, you went out of your way to make my presence known in Balitmore. I can't express to you how thankful I am for what you've done for me. You two deserve a standing ovation. Hugs and kisses. I love you.

Pam and PJ, you are the best in-laws. Thanks for all your help and support. If anybody got the word out about me, it was y'all. But what can I expect from the "Moses" of promoters and his wife? I love y'all.

Thank you to the rest of my family and friends for lending your support. Robert, Danyielle, David, Terrell, Tenika, Tiffany, Airis, Ajada, Kharla, Malikah, Teren—oh, and Teren, thanks for sharing your knowledge. Your degrees count for something (smile)—Aunt Paulette and Sean, Steve and Aunt Lisa, Jamal, Butch, Kevin, Aunt

Acknowledgments

Mary-Jane, Aunt Theresa, Aunt Kenyatta, Aunt Anna, Aunt Joanne, and the rest of the Haleys, Ms. Helena, the entire King family, Ms. Sheila, Ms. Debbie and Mr. David, Ms. Norma, Johnnita, and family, Mr. Bernie, Ms. Sue and Adiza, Ms. Phyllis, the St. Christopher's family, Ms. Marcia, Kelly, Art and Kia, Aunt Val, Angela and Kevin, Tillio and Tawanda and the rest of my ATL people, Ms. Robin, Aunt Rita, Nanna and the entire Augustine family, Nanny, Gus, and all the Colemans in Cleveland, Mom and Pop Cannon, Aunt Hope, my brothers- and sisters-in-laws, Jamal, Darnell, Phil, Al, Addrienne, Ashanti, Ashanta, and Keyani.

Thanks to Liza and Havis Dawson and everyone at Liza Dawson Associates; Cherise Davis, Meghan Stevenson, Jamie McDonald, Martha Schwartz, and everybody at Simon & Schuster; and Dawn Michelle and her team at Dream Relations. You all played very significant roles in getting this out promptly. Thank you for your hard work and dedication.

Thank you, Karen E. Quinones Miller and Daaimah S. Poole, for your generosity and all your help. I needed it. It's a blessing having people like you in my corner.

To other authors and friends—Omar Tyree, Brenda Thomas, Adrienne Bellamy, Shawna Grundy, Victoria Christopher Murray, Cydney Rax, Crystal Lacey Winslow, Mister Mann Frisby, and Nikki Turner—thanks for being so supportive of me and welcoming me to this industry with open arms.

Ed Crawford of Phatboy Media; Allen Stokes, Zachary Polland, and the Global Recording Group; Tiffany, Phyllis, and Wanda at Treo Models Inc.; Calvin

Acknowledgments

Childs of Calvin Childs Photography, thank you all for helping me with my hustle.

Thank you to everyone who has supported me and participated in any of my endeavors. I'm keeping it moving just for you.

Ya girl,

Miash